ABOVE
DISCOVERY

ABOVE
DISCOVERY

Jennifer Falkner

Invisible Publishing
Halifax & Toronto

Library and Archives Canada Cataloguing in Publication
Title: Above discovery / Jennifer Falkner.
Names: Falkner, Jennifer, author.
Description: Short stories.
Identifiers: Canadiana (print) 20220467080
        Canadiana (ebook) 20220467099
        ISBN 9781778430206 (softcover)
        ISBN 9781778430213 (EPUB)

Classification: LCC PS8611.A49 A86 2023 | DDC C813/.6—dc23

Edited by Bryan Ibeas
Cover and interior design by Megan Fildes | Typeset in Laurentian
With thanks to type designer Rod McDonald

Invisible Publishing is committed to protecting our natural environment. As part of our efforts, both the cover and interior of this book are printed on acid-free 100% post-consumer recycled fibres.

Printed and bound in Canada.

Invisible Publishing | Halifax & Toronto
www.invisiblepublishing.com

Published with the generous assistance of the Canada Council for the Arts, the Ontario Arts Council, and the Government of Canada.

For Chris and for Nick.

NINETEEN ABOVE DISCOVERY

AUGUST 31, 1896.

HERE, TO AVOID BEING POOR, we live worse than tramps, turning the earth inside out for gold.

Last night I dreamed we were back at Dyea, the first stop on our journey to the Klondike, still fresh and ignorant. We were dragging our outfit from the shallows where the boatmen had dumped it, racing the tide to get it to shore, then pitching our tent in a grove of cottonwoods, away from the dozen or so shacks that made up the town. Spring was late and the scene was nothing but shades of brown and grey. Except, in my dream, marking the trail into the woods—the trail that led up to that notch in the sawtooth mountains called the Chilkoot Pass—a forsythia stood in bloom. Its boughs glowed like gold.

Jack went back to the town site two days ago. He took the sled to return with more lumber and grub. We've been on the claim now for more than a month and the cabin's almost finished. We use three wooden crates for chairs and a table. In pride of place on the small shelf where we keep the tin plates and mugs, I placed my gold nugget. It was a gift from a cheery old prospector we passed on our way up Rabbit Creek. His claim was Eight Above Discovery and it looked like he'd been working it for ages. Several pits were dug into the muddy banks, and the sluice boxes seemed to be wicking gold straight out of the ground.

"Too many cheechakos up here, thinking bending over a creek with a pan's enough," the prospector said. "The cold may kill you, but the work won't." And he proffered a lumpen nugget as big as a robin's egg. I took it as a good omen. A talisman.

"You wouldn't recognize the place, Alma," Jack said. The town site, which six weeks ago was little more than a mudflat covered in alder and stunted willows, had been cleared. "It's like a circus come to the Klondike. You can barely see the ground for the grubby tents and shacks that have sprung up all over the place."

"Did you get any more bacon?"

"I got some lumber, that's it. And some tinned salmon. There are so many men and so few supplies. Already everything is too dear. We'll get by," he added, "as long as we're careful."

OCTOBER 28, 1896.

It snows every day, but lightly; there is little to clear. The pines on the hills look sparser now, something like the raised hairs on a man's arm. My days are mostly spent chopping them down. Jack scouts the claim, looking for the likeliest spot to start in earnest. In the long twilights the hills all around are dotted with bonfires, prospectors who've already started digging.

The Yukon is frozen over; there'll be no news or supplies from the outside until spring.

I keep thinking about that old sourdough back in Forty Mile. The one who gave me that nugget. His face barely visible beneath his grizzled whiskers. "You're fools if you listen to Carmack," he said. "There's no gold. I know those parts, and I tell you, the water in them creeks just don't taste right. You won't see any colour there."

DECEMBER 1, 1896.

Still no colour. Jack starts a bonfire every night and each morning. After we scrape away the ashes, he digs through the permafrost. He manages about a foot and a half per day. It would be more but for the blisters on his hands. I've been melting snow to pan through the muck he dredges up, and so far all I've found is an enormous quantity of black mud. This is our existence: pick and shovel, water and pan. Swishing water around the sediment, hoping some flakes of gold might separate and sink to the bottom. Day after day. Jack's been muttering about sinking another hole closer to the creek bed.

We get less than four hours of daylight now. In the long dusk, the land seems to turn on us, telling us we'll never be able to do all we have to do.

DECEMBER 5, 1896.

There is an argument brewing in our cabin. It's just been sitting there for weeks, but now it's inflating like a balloon, crowding out everything else. My nugget is missing. Jack blames me. He calls it a sign of my lazy housekeeping. He accuses me of spending too much time writing stories. He forgets that my little potboilers are what kept us going when Pa was ill.

I take long walks when the moon is full enough. The snow underfoot is pulverized sugar. I hike up to the highest hill, King Solomon's Dome, from which the ridges and valleys of the Klondike stem like spokes from the hub of a wheel. Silent fires dot the hills and blur the air with smoke. In many places the fires are hidden, the shafts sunk so deep that they look like pits leading to hell. No light, only heat and smoke pour out. There are ten claims to a mile here, they say, but only occasionally will I see another figure out here, bundled in furs against the wind. The land feels so empty.

On my return Jack never fails to ask in what direction I walked, how many windlasses I counted, how many claims, how big the dumps are. He can't stop thinking that everyone else is hitting pay dirt while we'll be lucky to break even. But for now I'm not speaking to him.

DECEMBER 10, 1896.

Snowing again. The sun doesn't show its face anymore, only gilds the hilltops around midday. The cabin is quiet. Jack and I barely speak. It's worse than when we were children. We sit in the gloom of our candles, breathing the sweet herbal smell of Jack's evening pipe, keeping company with our own thoughts.

DECEMBER 12, 1896.

Tonight, while I was frying up some flapjacks, Jack yanked Pa's watch right out of my pocket, as if he was grabbing a mouse by the tail. It was made from the silver Pa dug out of the mountain in Colorado, that watch, punched with fancy scrollwork and his favourite Latin motto, *tendit in ardua virtus*. Virtue strives for what is difficult. It hasn't worked since Alaska.

"What the hell, Jack?"

"I'm just taking what's mine. Since I'm the eldest. And the only surviving son. It belongs to me."

"And I get nothing? I looked after him. You got all his shares in the mine."

I tried to snatch it back. Soon we were rolling on the ground, spitting and screeching, no better than drunken brawlers on a Saturday night. We only stopped because our tussling knocked over the candle on the table.

Now Jack has a shiner on his cheek, and my ribs crackle when I breathe deep. But here's something: afterwards, when we were spent, lying in the dark on the hard dirt floor, I felt properly warm again.

"His debts," Jack said.

"What?"

"I didn't get his shares," said Jack. "I got his debts. There's nothing left."

Jack's probably right: Pa would have wanted him to have that watch. But it's the only lovely thing I own.

DECEMBER 25, 1896.

Christmas Day. Cold enough to harden quicksilver.

Yesterday we witnessed a rare specimen in these parts: a visitor. A chuckle-headed Swede in a red marten-skin cap, from two claims down. Nils Johansson. He came to invite us to dinner. And he lent me the snowshoes he was wearing for the journey. Unbuckled them then and there as we stood in the snow, waiting for Jack to climb out of the shaft. I've been living with my brother so long, I'd forgotten what gallantry was.

The Swede's cabin was small and filled with the fug of unwashed bodies. But he had one amenity: a window. It faced south and had no windowpane, but a dozen or so glass bottles filled the frame. Lord, but I envy him that window.

There was moose instead of turkey, and the only vegetables were hard little potatoes the size of Brussels sprouts, but there was conversation, and that was better than meat and drink. He had invited two more men, Artie Sloper and Hank Shaw from further down the creek, two sourdoughs who abandoned their claims near Forty Mile as soon as news of the strike here came in August. Their faces were dark and haggard, their bodies rail thin, and they spoke wildly of the fortunes they were digging out of the earth.

We didn't need the squeaky fiddles or the honky-tonk pianos of town. Artie grabbed my hand and swung me round the room, singing "Oh! Susannah." My sides ached from laughing so much. Then we sang "Good King Wenceslas," "The Bottom of the Punch-bowl," and wound up with a rather tearful "Auld Lang Syne." Prospectors are the most sentimental men you'll ever meet.

Jack didn't sing.

"What were you and Nils talking about?" I asked. "Thick as thieves you were all night."

"Hank's been seeing colour since before the freeze-up. Nils reckons they've got at least ten dollars a pan in their creek, maybe more."

When we got back, I found I'd forgotten to dump the old tobacco can I use as a chamber pot before we left, and its contents had frozen solid. I hurled it into the creek.

Terrible headache this morning.

JANUARY 6, 1897.

January and the logs of our cabin have shrunk, and most of the chinking has blown away from the never-ending wind. We re-pitched the tent and moved the bed and stove inside, leaving the cabin to shelter the tools and grub. Before Jack shovelled snow against them, the canvas walls puffed like a fat child out of breath. But for now the snow offers protection from the wind, except when one of us opens the flap and it pushes its way in, knives out, like a Colorado goon.

JANUARY 8, 1897.

The butter glides in circles around the pan as it sizzles and melts. It mirrors my thoughts, which keep returning to the same subjects: to spring, to the likelihood of a wasted year, to a life of poverty.

"Jack, perhaps we should consider selling the claim. We could use the money to find a likelier spot. Or just go home. Start again."

The bacon was frozen; I had to cut it into chunks outside with a hatchet. Now I dropped a large solid piece into the pan and jumped back from the spitting grease.

"It was a gamble, and it didn't pay off, that's all," I said, not turning round. "It happens every day. Pa used to say—"

"Just shut up about going home, will you? And shut up about Pa." He took a couple of steps, frustrated in his attempt to pace by the smallness of the tent.

"What's wrong with you?"

He picked up the hatchet I had brought inside and swung it randomly. I worried what he'd hit, the scant furniture we owned being the least of it. Cabin fever is a real thing and dangerous. It wasn't until he hurled the hatchet down so it became stuck in the ground that I breathed again.

He sat heavily on the bed and dropped his head into his hands. "I didn't pay his debts. The bank thinks we defaulted. We can't go back."

"So where's all the money? The money from the house?" I pried the hatchet from the floor and tucked it behind the table, out of sight.

"It paid for our outfit. We can't go back unless we've got at least twelve hundred dollars in our pockets. Even then, we'd barely break even."

The meat was starting to smoke and had blackened on one side. I turned it over with a fork, so at least the two sides would match.

He studied the floor as he spoke. "I didn't just want to pay Pa's debts. I thought we could make a fortune here. I just want this winter to end. I want—"

"A bath?"

"God, yes!" He sat up. "A bath. And proper grub. I want to eat till I burst."

I closed my eyes. "Roast beef, tomatoes, sweet peas. Chocolate."

"But no ices," he added, and I laughed. "Not even in our drinks. A soft feather bed. No more lumpy mattresses laid on spruce boughs." He grew serious. "Comfort, Alma. That's all. I want us to live in comfort. I'd do anything for that."

I lay my hand on his. It was warm, solid. That *us* would be worth more than all the gold in the Klondike—if I could hold him to it.

JANUARY 14, 1897.

Pa's watch is missing. It's not in the tent and I can't remember the last time I saw Jack with it. I asked, but he didn't seem bothered by its absence. I think he's hidden it somewhere, along with my nugget, maybe in order to feel like the claim holds at least some kind of wealth. It must be down there with him, but the relentless ring of his shovel hitting frozen earth warns me to leave him well alone.

Only halfway through January and already we're getting more daylight. Nearly six hours. But the cold doesn't budge.

FEBRUARY 3, 1897.

When I returned from my walk yesterday, Jack was darning his socks and humming an old romantic ballad I haven't heard since we left Colorado. He stopped when he saw me, both the humming and the sewing. There were snowshoe tracks leading to our camp. I didn't feel like asking and he didn't offer an answer.

FEBRUARY 7, 1897.

Seventy below, if the thermometer is to be believed. This morning I could hear my breath crackle as it hit the cold air. But it was my turn to collect wood for the stove. Jack stubbornly lay in bed. The wool blanket rippled over his body, covered in hoarfrost and looking like the hills and valleys outside.

It's only five or six steps from the tent to the woodpile. I thought at first my eyes were just sticky with sleep, but then it got so that after a few paces I couldn't open my eyes at all. I held my hands out to feel for the stacked logs, knocking several of them down by accident. I screamed.

Jack came running. "What? What is it?"

"I can't see!"

"For god's sake, Alma, don't cry! You'll make it worse." He led me by the arm back inside like I was an old woman. Under the annoyance, there was fear in his voice.

He sat me down on a crate before the stove.

"What is it? What's happening to me?"

Blindness was a disaster. Blindness meant being a burden. It meant the constant risk of abandonment, of giving up all hope of going home.

"Ice crystals. On your eyelashes. You'll be fine." He grasped my head with both hands and leaned close. "Hold still," he whispered. Two hot puffs of air, first one eye, then the other. A trickle of something like tears.

"Jack?"

"Yeah?"

"Can I open them now?"

"I think so. Just do it slowly, okay?"

"Okay." I tried to pretend I wasn't terrified.

And there he was, staring, anxious. I hugged him. How brotherly, to be so untrustworthy and so utterly reliable.

"I thought I told you not to cry."

"Can't help it."

"You better help it. I haven't got a clean handkerchief."

FEBRUARY 15, 1897.

The Swede dropped in, apparently to tell us he'd been snubbed by Hank and Artie. They're working hard at their claim and they either clam up whenever someone asks them about it or remark that the Yukon is filling up with gossips who'd do better to mind their own beeswax.

"That's them sorted then," said Jack. "The only question is how rich they are. Will they buy a hotel or a mansion?"

"Or maybe the governor's house?"

It was coming on to supper. "Coffee's run out," I said. Nils looked at Jack, who shrugged. I felt compelled to add, "But there's plenty of tea."

The tent was warm, and Nils removed his fur coat before perching on a crate. An inch of silver chain dangled from his trouser pocket.

I stood up, looked around foolishly, tried to speak, and sat down again.

"You all right, Alma?" said Jack.

"Yes. Fine. Perfectly fine, thank you."

He shot me a funny look.

Nils took his mug from Jack. "Of course, for all we know, we could all be richer than those two. They can't know more than we do until spring cleanup."

My watch. Jack had given it to the Swede. It was a love token, it had to be.

Jack was being very careful—he talked the way I've heard him talk to a hundred men—but Nils was easier to read. His smile shone like a glacier at sunrise, and he couldn't tear his eyes from Jack.

They talked about how soon the thaw could come, how they would go about constructing sluice boxes and harnessing water from the creek. Nils had never done it before, so Jack was in his element, describing how we did it in Colorado.

"The hardest part will be getting the lumber. It'll be a race to Ladue's mill come spring."

I see how it will be. They will leave together. They'll cross that infernal Yukon River back to the real world. I will be the spinster sister, a hanger-on. Not a partner anymore.

I'm glad there is so much emptiness here. It will make being alone easier to bear.

FEBRUARY 19, 1897.

Snow squalls have made it almost impossible to go outside. I am reduced to reading the labels on tins for diversion. Armour's Extract of Beef has never been so eloquent.

FEBRUARY 28, 1897.

Nils appeared early yesterday morning, hobbling into camp, his snowshoes nowhere to be seen. Moisture from his lungs when he exhaled had settled on his whiskers, coating his moustache and beard in ice, like insects in amber.

He was shivering and could barely get the words out. "Ice broke. It looked solid, the creek bed, but the ice broke, was too—too thin."

Jack took his arm and practically carried him to the stove. "Alma, get me a bucket of snow. We're going to have to rub it on his legs before we can warm him up."

"I can't feel my feet, Jack."

"Stupid man. Why didn't you build a fire?"

"Tried. Dropped the matches."

When I returned, Nils was calmer. Jack had fed him some whisky and cut the frozen moccasins from his feet. They were a ghastly colour, paler than a corpse.

Nils was mumbling now. "If you think that's best," he said.

"I do, Nils. We'll even do it now, so that when we get you to town, you don't have to worry about anything except getting better and going home. Alma, get me some paper from that notebook of yours."

He scribbled a handful of lines, then read them out. It was a deed of sale.

"Now you sign. One claim, Nineteen Above Discovery, for one nugget. That's got to be five hundred dollars right there." He pulled my nugget from his coat pocket, the same one he'd blamed me for losing. He didn't look at me.

"Good. Now Alma will sign too."

"Jack, what's going on?"

"Just doing Nils a favour. And it has to be in your name; we're only allowed one claim each. Get him a pair of my socks, will you? He's going to need them in a minute." He took the bucket and started rubbing handfuls of snow onto the Swede's feet.

They left early this morning. Jack settled Nils in the sled, tucked the blankets from his bed all round, and pulled him down to Artie Sloper's claim. Artie has dogs and can take him the rest of the way into town.

Jack hasn't come back yet.

MARCH 1, 1897.

Snowflakes drift down interminably. The empty tent was driving me mad, so I was out chopping firewood when Jack trudged back. Nils is gone. I followed Jack inside, where he dumped his blankets on the bed and sat by the stove.

"We're going to Seattle?"

Jack lit his pipe. "Of course not."

"I thought you and he—"

"Guess he realized how hard it would be working that claim alone with frostbit feet." His jaw was set.

"Jack, what happened?"

"Nothing happened! I bought us another claim, one right next to Shaw. It's got colour in it for sure and all you can do is nag. I did what you wanted me to. We're going to be rich."

He stormed off down to the creek.

MARCH 15, 1897.

The days are longer, but the cold remains intractable. Some days feel like an elaborate game of make-believe. It seems impossible that there is a fortune under all that muck. Or that the two of us could even extract it if there is.

The bags and wooden crates of supplies have dwindled and emptied. We have dried beans and flour. Nothing else, until the thaw.

There can be no looking back now, no remorse. Or we'll stay here forever.

NESTOR'S DREAM

WE'VE STOPPED AT LESSA. It's a straight road from here to Epidauros, but we have taken to travelling in shorter stretches, staying longer in the towns and villages along the way. Tedious but, at my age, necessary.

Where is Nestor? His sudden absences have become more frequent lately, more inopportune. He'll return eventually, when I'm famished and sunburned, when I've recorded every tattered rag of history this place can yield. And this temple is like a hundred others. Its wooden idol has so many roughly carved sisters across the Argolid. I made a joke to my guide about the goddess having an almost exact twin in the Temple to Hera in Nauplia. The young man, a junior priest by the looks of him, all oily hair and well-fed frame, didn't even smile.

There is so little here worth recording in my book, the *Guide*. A small village, an uneducated people, mainly farmers living at the foot of Mount Arachnaion. I've been told altars to Zeus and Hera lie farther up the mountain, places these people go to sacrifice in times of drought, but they hardly seem worth the effort of a visit. Instead, I continue to pick my way around the Temple to Athena, the one interesting spot in Lessa. My sandal leather is grass thin, and the rough stones try their best to pierce it. I really must get Nestor to take them to a decent cobbler.

Only a handful of people here. A couple of priests, a few ancient women draped in black, the same crows picking among the stones you can see everywhere. The temple precinct was paved once, but time, earthquakes, and poverty have left the ground a rough blanket of rubble. The cicadas keep to their monotonous song under the livid sun. There is the scent of wild thyme and occasionally a bee that seems to erupt from the stony earth itself.

There is that boy again, coming out of the temple. I didn't like the look of him on sight, and judging from his scowl, nor did he like me. Some apprentice priest, perhaps. I remember the boredom of being that age and how quickly it could give rise to cruelty. He's spotted me before I can reach the shade of the wild olive grove beyond the temple and hide.

He apes my uneven gait, a mocking shadow. Now that he's closer, gaining on me, I can see he's older than I thought, closer to fourteen. My eldest grandson's age. Only this boy is uglier, leaner, fiercer. Lucius, the last time I saw him, still had dimples when he smiled.

No sign of any priests now. Even the crow women have taken flight. I am alone with the boy.

I stop, turn, and face him, scowling. He's in mid-step, his arms outstretched, pretending to be as off-balance as I am. He stares back, unabashed.

Long seconds pass and I am afraid, truly afraid. A mere boy. But, with no one here, he could do anything he wants to me. This is what it is to be old.

I must give up my plan of sitting in the shade until Nestor—where is he?—returns. So often now, after a morning of exploring, my legs become so stiff that after I sit to rest them, I need Nestor's help to stand again. I would be as foolish as a field mouse sauntering before an owl if I were to sit down now.

I turn away from the grove, away from the boy, and back to the road we came in on, the straight road that will take us to Epidauros, and there, to my delight, to my relief, I can see Nestor. More tanned than when we left home two years ago, greyer too, slightly stooped, but who am I to question the form of my salvation? He's carrying something, which, knowing Nestor, is likely to be a flask of wine, along with some bread and cheese wrapped in cloth. In other words, lunch.

I raise my hand, call his name, though my voice is more gulping and frail than I would like. But I don't care. I can show my fear now that it is ebbing. The boy spits at the ground near my feet so I can be in no doubt of his contempt before he turns away.

By the time Nestor is close enough, I am more in command of myself. "Any news?"

Beneath his tan, Nestor almost looks pale. Too pale for this heat. "A merchant can take us to Epidauros tomorrow. Nothing today. There was a story of an oracle, a human-headed snake, but I think it's too new for you. Only about fifty years old," he says.

"There's so little around here that I might have to use it. But I'm not desperate yet."

We can sit in the shade now. I swallow a mouthful of wine. It is sharp, almost acidic. I hope Nestor didn't notice the boy. I hope he wasn't witness to my humiliation.

-->>)((<--

The following day, they stop at the sanctuary of Asklepios, just outside Epidauros. Nestor finds a guide, another young priest who can take his master through the sanctuary, point out the paintings, the important architecture, tell the stories of the place. Perhaps even show him the idol of Asklepios himself, reported to be made of gold and ivory. And with his master fixed up for at least a couple of hours, he's on his own.

The sanctuary is enormous. Myrtle and thyme, sweet marjoram and bergamot, they grow plentifully, crawling with bees along the pathways. It must be convenient, having all the ingredients for garlands and crowns for festival time grown all in one place. He passes marble statues of Sleep, of Drunkenness. Young men, louche, carefree. He can't remember that kind of irresponsibility. It must have been delightful. Then Hygeia and Epione. Upright women both, concerned with health, with recovery. Always the women cleaning up the messes of men.

And finally, Asklepios himself. God of Healing.

He is a stocky god. The locks of his oiled hair and beard writhe like snakes across the painted marble. They make Nestor think of the yellow snake sunning itself on his stone seat outside the Temple to Athena yesterday, back in Lessa. While his master daydreamed, gazing out at the bees and butterflies, he was transfixed by the snake's uncanny undulation across the hot surface.

Now, beyond the baths and the race course, which today lie empty, he finds what he's looking for. His head aches from the sun. The dryness in his mouth tastes something like dread. But it's too late to turn back.

One of the men sitting outside the long, low building, resting on the wooden bench in the shade, has a goitre ballooning from his throat, a goitre so large he can't turn his head left or right but must rotate his whole torso to look around him. He gestures to Nestor, waves him nearer. He has a sprig of rosemary pinned to his tunic, another tucked over his ear.

"You're new," he says.

His voice is soft. Nestor can barely make it out. He wonders what it feels like, the fleshy ball erupting from his throat. Does it press on his windpipe like a murderous hand?

"If you're here to stay the night, to have the god visit your dreams, you have to see Biton." The man jerks his thumb to a knot of men a few yards away. "He's in charge of intake."

Nestor slips him a coin in thanks.

Biton could be mistaken for a bricklayer. Short, sturdy, thumbs hooked into his belt. But Nestor doesn't know how to interrupt, to insert himself into this man's notice. He'll have to come back later. His master will be finished with his tour soon, ready to move on to the city proper. Nestor still needs to find them rooms for the night and a reputable place to eat.

-»»×««-

Epidauros, named for one of the sons of Apollo, contains much worth visiting (a phrase dearly loved by guide writers). A Sanctuary of Aphrodite. Temples dedicated to Dionysus and Artemis. An impressive theatre and odeon. And down near the harbour, a Temple to Hera, queen of the gods. Almost overwhelming after Asklepios's sleepy sanctuary. I will have to get down there with my notebook.

The thing I try to capture for the *Guide* isn't necessarily the monument itself. Not the temple or theatre or tomb. It's not even the stories of heroism that make the stones significant for having been witnesses to them, though I am particular in my research and retelling. It is the part that is missing that I am drawn to, that I try to pin down. My gaze is always divided by what is here and what is no longer here. That, for me, is where the deepest pleasure lies, where the sweet overcomes the bitter. The pleasure of loss, after time has passed.

My gaze now slides past the statues at the agora's entrance. Roman generals, mostly. Figures I may safely ignore. Along with their emperors. So many Augustuses, Tiberiuses and Trajans. The paint is still fresh on Hadrian and his philosopher's beard. I may be forced to live here in this modern world, under the rule of a Roman emperor, but no one can compel me to preserve it in my work. The past, the *Greek* past, is by far a worthier place to visit.

A chance encounter with a pretentious banker leads me to an introduction with the local governor. Demetrios. He may have been educated in Rome, but that's hardly his fault. He is a true Greek. A man of enthusiasms: for sport, for racing, for theatre, for history. And, most of all, for performance.

"You must give us a reading of your work. Tonight, at the odeon. I'll arrange it. How lucky we are to have a modern Herodotus visit our city. And you must stay with us too. My wife will be thrilled to have such a distinguished guest in our house."

I doubt that very much. My own wife was seldom thrilled by unexpected company, distinguished or not. And I am certainly no Herodotos, though I've read his *Histories* so often, especially during my travels, that my scrolls are crumbling and stained in places. Two scrolls were lost during an overnight transfer of luggage on our passage to

Corinth, and I still haven't been able to replace them.

But it is so gratifying to find someone who appreciates my work, who sees what I am trying to achieve, that his invitation is impossible to refuse. A complete *Guide to Greece*. To its every region. A compilation of cities and monuments and legends. A record of battles and stories of heroes. A map in words. A pilgrimage made through reading. Nestor thinks me mad.

But a public reading? I remember how little my speeches back in Magnesia could hold an audience. However carefully planned, at the last minute, my own words would throw up traps for my tongue. The audience would titter as I stumbled. And my wife, coiffed and perfumed for public engagements, practised insincerity in her praise. She was already saving her true smiles for someone else.

→→→)(←←←

The first doctor Nestor consulted, back in Magnesia, said it was the result of an imbalance, of too much black bile. That's what caused the burning sensation at night around his heart and up into his throat. Eat more pulses, the doctor said. And prop your head and shoulders up at night with more pillows.

And the dizziness? Oh, said another, this time in Delphi, that's the result of too much phlegm. Eat fewer pulses and rest more, take small naps during the day.

What about the tingling in his hands and feet? The leaden feeling in his chest sometimes, as if he were being pressed by a stone? His sudden breathlessness? The times when the corridors of his body rush with a sudden heat and his skin feels licked by flames?

The third doctor, an Athenian, looked grave, checked the colour and texture of his tongue. Twice. "You might try a full immersion in the healing springs during one of these attacks. Failing that, have you considered dream incubation?"

Nestor's face crimped with impatience.

Biton has assigned him a bed. He said with the proper purification ritual in the pool, Nestor can forgo the traditional three days' fast.

He's not sure if he trusts the young doctor-priest. It seems unlikely his cure could be found in dreams, even in this sacred place. Mostly he just dreams of home anyway. But he is sick of pulses. Naps are impossible as long as his master wants to wander. And he will throttle the next man to prescribe him a course of laxatives. He is so tired. This malfunction of his body is beginning to feel like less of a betrayal. It has become a part of him now. Perhaps he should just accept it.

A man on the cot next to his cries out in his sleep. "Talos! Talos!" he screams, as if he is actually being crushed by the bronze automaton of legend whose metal body contains a furnace, who kills his enemies with a scalding embrace. A young priest kneels by his head, murmurs soothingly. He wipes the man's skin with a cloth dipped in cool water while the man's body debates with death. It overcomes him by turns with fieriness and with shivering.

"Don't worry," says the priest, seeing Nestor staring. "Nobody dies here. It's forbidden, at least within the sanctuary."

The blanket rasps as Nestor pulls it up over his ear to block out all the noises of the room. He squeezes his eyes shut. He tries not to think of all the ill and dying men the blanket has warmed before. He tries not to think of its likely fleas. Or bedbugs. Already there is an itch on his leg. Is that a blasphemous thought, that there could be bedbugs in a place sacred to a god?

Nestor, exhausted, sleeps.

He hears them before he can see them.

A humming murmur, a rising growl. A fast-flowing cloud, a swarm of bees. They are aiming for the pine tree ahead of him—he is directly between them and it—and for a moment, for seconds, an eternity, they surround him. Swarming, crawling, tickling, pinching. He is, for a moment, one of them, part of their energetic stream, one of the thousand lives that make up one life.

And then, just as suddenly, they are gone. Flown past, moved on. And Nestor's ears are stuffed with silence.

-⇥⇥✖⇤⇤-

Success! Glory! Triumph! Oh, I am loved. I am *loved* here. The audience, they clapped and clapped. They wanted more; I could tell. I read to them from my manuscript, read to them about Athens, about Delphi. Their heads all tilted forward to listen more closely. I took them on a journey with me to those places. Later Demetrios made me promise to send him a copy of the entire *Guide* when it's completed. If only my wife could know of this.

It is night down by the harbour, down past the governor's residence, past Hera's Temple, and I am dancing. Dancing! I should be too old for this. But I'm not. I could have had a litter return me to my lodging, but I declined. This feeling in my chest, it's too large to be contained in a litter or by four walls and a ceiling. I need to be here, by the water. And I want for no witnesses, really, not even my wife. I am happy. Adored. And the stars are magnificent. The gods have leaned down to see my joy, and I could brush them with my fingers if I reach up only a little higher.

Everything is so close, so precious. The black water lapping, the fishing boats nuzzling together. The sound of my feet dancing on the gravel shore.

I know I am no Herodotos. Nestor will still think me mad, still think I should be enjoying my retirement at home. To him, being so far from home is a punishment. No, I am not Herodotos. I can't map the known world. But I can be somebody else. Somebody new.

It isn't nostalgia that prompts me to write, as some have claimed. This isn't a simple celebration of the past in the face of a present in decline. No! It's a revolt against the strictures of the present. These men, my audience, these citizens of Epidauros. They're my fellow revolutionaries!

-->>)(<<-

The coughing begins after the moon has set. Near dawn, the patient next to him hacks up some ripe matter, which the attending doctor-priest, one Nestor hasn't seen before, examines with fascination. Nestor's eyes close again. When they open, it is morning; the patient is gone, the cot stripped.

A new priest moves along the rows. He possesses a kind of grace, a kind of lightness. Nestor has to bite back his envy. If he could only have this man's youth, his lightness. He thinks he had it once. But maybe it too was a dream.

The young priest, called Phrontis, makes note of Nestor's temperature, his pulse, his dream. It is really only the dreams that are important here. Nestor braces himself for the prescription of another laxative.

Phrontis doesn't soften his words, though his tone is gentle. He is not cruel, but Nestor feels bludgeoned. Suffocated. Already part of the buried world.

-->>)(<<-

I wake in the plain, whitewashed room of the inn. Wisps of a dream. The irrecoverable past. My wife's dimples. Her laughter. They seep back into the blankets, the blank walls, into the sounds of another morning. The gulls outside are hungry. There is the creak of wooden wheels, the voices of men getting ready for work. I pull my blanket higher, and my toes are naked in the cold air. My head aches. Too much wine. As it does almost every morning, my mind races back to the memory of the priest at Delphi, the one who refused me entry, who said I was not important enough to see the oracle. He took my money anyway. Barely disguising a mocking smile. Charlatans, all of them, these priests, these oracles. This is what old age is. I passed the Altars of Pity, Shame, Rumour, and Impulse as I made my way back to our lodgings. I came so close that day to just going home.

It is a fantasy, this land I describe. I have always been an unreliable narrator. Even more so when I drink too much.

As I lean out the window, looking down into the inn's peristyle, its pear trees, its pots of myrtle, hoping the air will clear my head, Nestor knocks and enters, bearing a tray. Ah, breakfast.

COLUMBINA

WHEN A PUPPET STOPS BREATHING, the audience holds its breath. It's one of those unconscious things; even I can't help it after all these years. For a moment the air doesn't move. Nothing moves. There is no sound but the soft clicking of my watch. Then the lights go down and, heart knocking against my chest, I gulp for breath and step toward the applause.

No one comes to these shows to see a new story. Everyone knows Hansel and Gretel, Cinderella, Faust. They come to marvel at the marionettes, to watch something mechanical turn into something alive. The pumpkin becomes a coach, the poor scholar becomes a rich man.

All my shows are dumbshows—I don't have Gillespie's talent for voices—but they're as choreographed as ballets. They're almost as real.

Gil took me on as a kind of apprentice, though he could barely cobble together a living by himself. His parade of puppets was the only thing that made sense after my mother died. I followed them to the park or the public library on Johnson Street, his puppet shows about how the tiger became striped or why the hare has such long ears.

There's a church around the corner from the theatre. A small gothic stone building with red-painted doors. They're propped open tonight and the sound of the choir spills into the evening.

Bread of heaven, bread of heaven
Feed me now and evermore
Feed me now and evermore

I know this hymn. I stood next to my mother on sun-soaked Sunday mornings, inflating my lungs to complete the long line. I remember the ache, the breathlessness. The melody follows me as I turn the corner, as I scan the faces of the men outside the homeless shelter, as I walk the few blocks home and struggle with my key. I'm inside before I realize the words have changed.

Breath of heaven, breath of heaven
Leave me now and evermore
Leave me now and evermore

-->>)(((-

I have given shows about Medusa turning men to stone, and Daphne escaping Apollo by becoming a laurel tree.

But I have an idea for a new metamorphosis, this time from Shakespeare. A pun on my name. "It is the owl and not the lark." At least, I think that's the line. It doesn't matter. It's the change that matters.

Before I do anything else—change out of my black stage clothes or grab a handful of cereal—I reach for my notebook and sketch: a girl getting ready for bed. She's brushing her long hair, draping a nightgown across the end of the bed. As she raises her floor-length dress over her head, talons instead of feet are revealed, tawny feathers instead of skin. As she pulls it over her head, large round eyes and a sharp yellow beak appear. She hops once, twice, then flies out of the open window, only to reappear a moment later silhouetted against a silver moon. When she returns, she perches on the dressing table, a limp mouse clutched in her beak.

-➤➤❭❬❬❮-

I was eighteen when I joined the corps of the Royal Winnipeg Ballet. I was twenty-one when I came back home, a torn meniscus and two surgeries later. My mother didn't know what to do with me. She tempted me with shopping on Princess Street, matinees at the Screening Room. I was invited to every board-game night with her friends. I think I made her a little crazy.

Then she came home with Columbina. She had found her in an antique store, trailing broken strings from head and hands. The small figure, barely ten inches high, in her old-fashioned diamond-patterned dress with its yellowed lace collar and cuffs, would have been part of a set, my mother said, based on figures from *commedia dell'arte*. Harlequin and Pierrot and the rest. It was amazing she had survived in such good condition.

There is a residue of life in old marionettes: in their unmoving faces, their blocky, unnatural hands. The people who manipulated them and their emotions still haunt the dolls. This kind of theatre is considered a debased art, childish. But really it is more subversive than that. The puppeteer is a sibling to the fire-eater, the tightrope walker, more akin to the freakish world of the circus than the respectable world of ballet. I don't think my mother knew quite what she had done.

Gillespie appeared around the same time Columbina did. A friend of a friend of a friend from school, a volunteer at the library, introduced us. At least ten years older than me, with curly dark hair and a grin like a puppy's wagging tail, he didn't have the desperate discipline you usually see in someone trying to make a living from art. After a lifetime of dance, I was ready to live without discipline.

He taught me how to re-string Columbina, how to make her walk and wave to the audience. Unlike a dancer, a puppeteer cannot control each limb independently. She must yield to its weight, its momentum, its pendular swing, to convince an audience. Her gaze can never leave the marionette she controls; her concentration sends her soul down her hands and fingers to the strings and into the doll itself. It's not like dancing; it's like possession. Soon Columbina could waltz into a room, she could flirt and laugh and tell bawdy jokes. She danced frenetically when the spirit moved her.

Gil tried to work with Columbina too sometimes, but she wanted nothing to do with him. He pulled her strings to lift her head, to raise her arms into fifth position, and though she obediently chasséd across the stage when prompted, her movements were derisive, her eyes rebellious.

-»>«<-

I didn't remove any of my mother's things when Gillespie moved in, so the house got a little crowded. Clothing racks dominated the living room, dripping with marionettes like overburdened Christmas trees. Gil helped fill the silence. He also filled the sink with dirty dishes, the bathroom with noxious smells, and the blue bin with beer cans. I needed the company too much to complain.

As he unpacked, I stood in front of the stereo with Columbina; she was dancing the dying swan. It was supposed to be sad, and it was easy to start weeping. It wasn't so easy to stop. Gillespie took the wooden control from my hands, laid Columbina on the floor, keeping her strings straight, and pulled me into his arms, holding me so tightly his shoulder dug into my neck and I couldn't breathe. I pushed at his chest, pulled out of his arms, while he—confused—held on too long, too tightly. It threw me off balance and I stumbled. My weight landed on Columbina, my bare heel on her skirt. Like the sound of a needle dragging across a record, that tearing of cloth, as I turned and fell.

"Look what you've done!"

"Lark, I'm sorry. It was an accident."

I took a deep breath. "It's fine. No, it's fine."

Columbina never liked Gillespie. She'd make fun of his walk or ape his gestures when his back was turned. Her wooden limbs would rattle and he'd turn suddenly, only to find her feet swaying in a non-existent breeze. Or she'd make faces when he wasn't looking. But whenever he turned to see what I was grinning at, her features were as wooden as ever.

But I never thought he'd actually leave.

-->>>){(<--

Every night it takes a good hour or more to fall asleep. Sometimes getting ready for bed feels like getting ready for battle. Tonight I don't even bother. I sit cross-legged on the bedroom floor, with several small blocks of seasoned oak and all my chisels in easy reach. Who needs a workshop? All I need is newspapers spread on the floor to catch the shavings. I start with her taloned feet.

I was his apprentice for a year and a half, but I haven't seen him in three. The puppet community is small; when I'm occasionally asked about him, I say, "Oh, he moved to Toronto." Or Montreal. Or New York.

If anyone were to question me about his watch, conspicuous on my thin wrist, I would say, "He left it behind," or "It was a parting gift." But so far no one has. I was going to pawn it, but I like its weight. The reliability of its movement, its unrelenting ticking. And how much could this old military watch be worth, really, with its plain black face and dirty canvas strap?

The Lark-puppet's hands are human and not too difficult to fashion. I've done enough of them over the years. They always look somewhat blocky, but I know I can make them graceful once they're strung. Like the papier-mâché head, they'll be attached to the dress, so when she pulls it off, head and hands will disappear into the bundle of fabric.

The wood is smooth, its sharp fragrance soaks into my fingers. I start the owl's head, pulling the chisel down the grain, roughing out its staring eyes. The beak has to be sharp enough to grip the dead mouse. A smaller chisel will give the impression of feathers before I detail the rest in paint.

Gillespie was with me the night my mother died. In moments like those you're supposed to gaze into the person's face, to read it for signs of love and farewell. But she was already unconscious, her face tilted toward the empty window, slack-jawed, straining to breathe. I stared instead at her breast, at the ridiculous fruit print of the thin cotton sheet that covered it. I knew the exact moment it happened. Though her ragged breathing had stopped, still for a moment or two the fabric covering her stubborn heart kept pulsing. Like a clock winding down.

Then it stopped.

Gillespie held my hand. And I held my breath.

-»>»<«-

It was a preposterous choice of fabric for a marionette, patterned with cherries and bananas and apples far too large for the tiny body. One banana was as long as Columbina's thigh. An apple could eclipse her entire head. But the diamond pattern on her old dress would have been as jewel-bright as this when it was new. I was half-buried in a nest of fabric scraps in the middle of the couch. Poor nude Columbina lay on the coffee table, staring blankly at the ceiling. Her torso, never meant to be exposed, was rough-hewn. You could see the chisel marks made by the original carver, like a potter's fingerprints on the bottom of a vase. When Gil came in, I pulled a scrap over her to protect her modesty.

"I'm making her a new dress."

"So I see. The other one's ruined then?" His tone was even, careful. Columbina and I exchanged a look.

"She wanted something new."

He was already backing out of the room. The snips and scraps of cotton fell from my legs, moulting feathers, when I rose to follow. I found him in the bedroom, shoving clothes into his bag.

"What are you doing?"

"I'm sorry," he said, not looking up.

I hung in the doorway hesitantly.

"I can't do this anymore. I'm not ... equipped." He looked at me then. "You talk to that marionette like she's real."

"I'll stop if you want me to. I'm not crazy. You know I'm not."

"There are people who can help, who specialize. Grief counsellors—"

That word was like a starting gun. I was already halfway down the hall.

"Lark! We've talked about this—"

It took less time than I expected for him to box up his puppets, his marionettes. The clowns, the magicians, the kings and queens. Only Columbina remained. By the time the street lights came on, he was gone.

I keep looking for him; I scan every crowd for his face. But if I did see him again, what could I say? He and Columbina could never live under one roof.

THE ANCHORESS

LAUDS

SOMETHING HAS ENTERED THE CHURCH. Something that makes claw-like clicks along the tiled floor of the nave.

The door must have been left open after evensong. Easy to do—the door is heavy and difficult to pull tight.

She rises from her narrow bed to look through the squint, the narrow opening that allows her to view the sanctuary—the stone altar with its two thick candles, the wooden cross on the wall behind. When the candles are lit, the cross appears to tremble in their plumes of heat. Sometimes she wishes the squint were a little wider, that she could see the images painted on the plaster walls along the nave. Green tendrils under the haloed saints and all the flowers of Paradise. Her memory of them is not strong.

There's a fox in the church. A vixen, her red fur smeared with grey. She is too thin—her ribs show plainly. She has gone as far as the three pillars that separate the nave from the chancel, sniffs around the base of one of the pillars. What does she smell? The odour of sanctification? Has she detected the rotting relics of Saint Balthild—a desiccated toe, a fragment of skull—hidden within the narrow pillar? Certainly not enough for a meal. The vixen looks up, looks at the back wall of the church, suddenly, sharply. She knows she is being watched.

The anchoress can't call anyone. The church is too isolated. And she doubts how far her thin voice, surrounded by four stone walls, could even travel. There is nothing to be done. She can only watch. And pray. Thank goodness it is only a fox. What if thieves came and helped themselves to the church's humble treasures—the silver chalice, the small gold cross Father Ambrose swears came from Rome?

The fox sniffs each pillar in turn, then circles back to the first one, Saint Balthild's resting place. She squats down onto her haunches and takes a shit.

The anchoress, watching alone from her cell, bursts into laughter.

PRIME

Her cell hugs the little stone church. It is spare but comfortable. She has a narrow cot along one wall, a small fireplace on another, with firewood stacked neatly beside it. The earthen floor is softened by rush mats that give off a summer sweetness when she treads on them. She has her own little flint and tinderbox to light the oil lamp, a book of

Hours and a book of Rules. She is a solitary bee in a lonely hive. Her day is broken into prayer and study and work. She mends Father Ambrose's shirts or makes tunics for the poorer families of the parish.

She has a single wall hanging, suspended over the cell's door. It helps with the drafts. It also helps her forget about the nails holding the door closed behind it, of the last words she heard before they were hammered in: "Deliver me, O Lord, from death eternal on that fearful day, when the heavens and the earth shall be moved, when thou shalt come to judge the world by fire." *Timor mortis conturbat me.*

The hanging is one she embroidered. The image is from Genesis, Adam and Eve in the Garden. She had difficulty with the people, but the trees, the flowers, the creatures of the ground, and the birds of the air she could pick out in detail easily. Sometimes, when she rises in the darkness for Matins or Lauds, the small light offered by her lamp animates the cloth. Swallows course across the dome of the sky, shrews and rabbits scurry through the green and yellow undergrowth.

When she kneels beneath the simple cross affixed on the wall above her squint, knees fitting into the gentle grooves of her stool, she can see glimmers from the candlelight. After mass, sometimes the smoke from the candles rises and spreads like a veil. Beyond the veil hangs the larger cross, the one from Rome. It seems encrusted with rubies, but only the sunlight filtering through the stained glass makes it appear so.

Usually, the silence is wide. It is gracious. It receives the birdsong, the rustling of leaves and grasses, rain when it falls on the roof tiles, the choir's reedy voices, the wagons rumbling over the rutted track. It embraces them. Embraces her.

TERCE

The only window to the outside world is supposed to be too high for her to see out. Or for others to see in. But if she stands on her bed, her toes balanced on its wooden frame, she can peel back the cotton fabric tacked across its opening and see the broad green track.

There it lies, the track that diverges from the Icnal Way, separating the field from the woods. Strange that this thing, this accident of landscape and travellers' feet, enticed her like a ribbon seller at market. Beckoned and flirted with her along hilltops and down valleys. It is such a still, unmoving thing now. There it lies, as still as she lies upon her bed at night.

She cannot see the yew whose shadow falls over the track, though she can see the red berries it drips, attracting birds and children. The only part of the tree that isn't poisonous. The yew, older than the church itself, marks a meeting place, they say, for the people who lived here even before the Romans. Weapons are not allowed in its shade, so it has always been a place of safety. The shadows from its long, pendulous branches move like weeds under water, slowly, slowly, sadly.

She prays for her mother's soul as she was instructed to do. She wonders if her father is still living. She prays for his as well, in case he is not. She prays for the villagers, that they may be preserved from sickness, that all their babes are delivered safe and well. She prays for the crops. As she prays, she can see, tucked under the warm soil, the barley seeds splitting, unfurling, sending roots deeper into the earth. She prays for the weather, for the wind that drives clouds and cold across the sky. For the swallows that swoop and circle, for the plate-faced owls at dusk. For the bees and beetles and butterflies. Twitchy-nosed rabbits and mice, and all creatures that burrow in the ground. She prays for all these things. Sometimes she wonders if she is praying to them.

SEXT

A man's voice. A stranger. He is under her window, talking with Father Ambrose, and when his voice isn't obscured by the wind rising like waves through the trees, she can hear him. A man who would not be blown away in a storm. Father Ambrose is recounting tales of Saint Balthild and her miracles. Then he speaks of the anchoress herself—another woman immured. He speaks of her as if she is his property, his source of miracles, his pet.

The stranger's reply is at first indecipherable. Almost as if he is speaking English with a mouth full of pebbles. The vowels are too rounded, then the consonants rise up like thistles, in all the wrong places.

She sees him on Sunday as he assists Father Ambrose with the service. He leads the meagre congregation in prayer. He has the stocky build of a farmer.

He kneels under her squint and asks her to pray for him. His voice is low and pleasant. "I am the first to visit you. But others will come. They will be moved by your piety."

"I am not a saint."

"And yet you have blessed me."

"How?"

Instead of answering, he tells her of his travels in the East, of women in the desert who also live alone, withdrawn, who also dedicate themselves to God.

But she does not feel withdrawn from anything. The world still assails her.

He tells her of the plague that has spread through Rome, through Constantinople and Jerusalem. Everywhere God is angry, he says. But not here, not in this land.

Maybe He is, she wants to say. *One voice alone is a tyrant. But here He is only one voice among many. And there are so many gods.* But she is reluctant to say so much.

"How did you come to be here?"

"My father sent me." She doesn't say that a sickly child with a split and twisted lip and overly prominent front teeth, grown into an ugly daughter, is not a difficult sacrifice to make. *I am his silence, his prayers and contemplation. He can run the business, oversee the lands and the household, because of me.*

Meanwhile the jackdaws are clamouring into the sky.

NONE

Mostly she eats pottage made from cabbage and onion and leeks. Sometimes Mary, her servant, flavours it with thyme or rosemary and thickens it with barley. Plums and medlars in late summer. Bread and honey. Once Mary brought her rabbit in a stew. She stirred in the thick skin congealed over the top. It was barely warm after travelling so far from Mary's kitchen. The taste, the texture of flesh, was strange after long abstinence. The anchoress forced herself to chew, forced herself to swallow. For three days after, her belly was in spasms and refused all food. She was hot and clammy at once, curled on the hard floor next to her bed. In her delirium she was troubled by foxes and hares; they chased and chased her around the church. The foxes' claws clattering like hailstones on the roof. The hares, all stretched ears and protruding yellow teeth, grotesque, frightening.

Mary's visits also bring news. As she passes a basket of food through the narrow opening or takes away a chamber pot, she always has some tidbit to share. The storm destroyed the pea crops. Birds were killed and branches knocked off trees by hailstones as big as hens' eggs. The stranger who boasted he was a giant-killer and had the leg bone of a giant as proof and charged a penny to see it. But it was clearly an ox bone and though the man denied it, he did not stay in the village long. A thief, a boy known by his clipped ear, was hanged. Father Ambrose prayed for him but insisted he still had to answer for his crime on earth.

She clips her hair short whenever it becomes long enough to twirl around her finger. The clumps that fall on her lap, that she collects and places on the windowsill for the birds to use in their nests, are more grey than brown now, stiff, almost brittle.

VESPERS

Her knees have begun to ache when rain is coming. Her knuckles swell in the cold, and she can no longer hold her needle. She sleeps less and less.

Then, just as the stranger said they would, the pilgrims come. At first, only a trickle, then in a torrent. They converge on the Icnal Way, on the green track to Saint Balthild's, wearing their many badges—souvenirs of other pilgrimages—loudly broadcasting their adventures or giving each other advice on the best roads, the cleanest and cheapest inns. All of them want to visit her.

One claims she cured his blindness. Another her lameness. Stories of withered limbs restored, barren wombs made fertile. How ridiculous they are. These pilgrims, if they can't have a badge, must at least have a miracle. Of course she has done nothing but pray. Of course they believe what they want to believe.

She keeps the little door closed now. Mary's daughter has to knock when she comes with food or clean linen. It is harder and harder to find her silence.

Thick plumes of pearly smoke come up from the village every day.

And more come. God must be angry in this land now too, for there is a contagion spreading through the village. A putrid fever, a cough. Death is swift and not merciful. She can hear on the wind the bell tolling at the monastery three miles away. Saint Balthild's has no bell. But it does have lamentations and hymns and prayers. It has the sound of shovels hitting the earth, shifting the ground. Father Ambrose says the cemetery sprouts graves like dandelions. For a while the church, and he, are busier than ever.

COMPLINE

Then they went. The pilgrims no longer come. Mary's daughter no longer stops to chat. The church feels hollow. Her cell is too warm.

Her prayers are falling away. She can no longer hold the words in her mind. Only the curlews piping somewhere over the downs. Only the crickets' song and the rising and falling of wind tides in the yew's long branches. She's troubled; she begs forgiveness of God. God or her father. Both of them. Neither.

She slips to her knees at the appointed hours, her prayer book open to the correct page. Her body obedient, while her soul, it seems, flies up and out of the tiny cell, sweeps through the wide sky like a spring wind. When she neglects to take the Eucharist from the priest through the small window, he hisses at her, "Are you sick? Are you dead?"

If she isn't there to pray for her mother's soul, to pray for the village, their crops, then why is she there? What is a woman who chooses to be alone?

A monstrous thing.

Mary's daughter—or is it her granddaughter now?—brings her fresh linens with a sprig of lavender tied to the top coverlet. All morning she contemplates its many flowers; they are like eyes gazing all around itself. She imagines what it sees when it looks around the whitewashed walls, what it remembers of fields upon fields of fellow blooms: the tickling scurry of ants and beetles up its stem. The penetration of busybody bees. Rabbits bounding through its patch, their noses wrinkling and flaring as they stop to nibble at its sweetness.

And everything she has prayed for, everything she has prayed to, is with her now. The silence is full of songs. They are sung by her mother, sister, daughter, the sun and moon, the trees pushing up to the sky, the birds swooping down to the earth.

And they are closer to me than I am to myself.

The stone walls of her cell, two halves of an eggshell, crack open.

MATINS

A blackbird sounds out the dawn.

The dew is heavy on the grass by the church wall, but grey-brown fur protects her from the damp. She lifts her head, her nose twitching as she tests the cool air for its trails of scent. The church still lies in shadow, but unmistakably the sun is rising on the land.

What is a hare that chooses to be alone?

One of God's many creatures.

She nibbles on a long stalk, then, as the shadow of an owl darkens the grass, hops into the shade of a tree and out of sight.

LION IN THE DESERT

MEMORIES TUMBLE LIKE THE LEAVES OUTSIDE, an onslaught of colour and sadness.

You, laughing, guiding the steering wheel with one wrist. The tails of my scarf, tied Audrey Hepburn–style under my chin, blown into my mouth by the hot wind when I couldn't stop talking of the potsherds we found that day, the mudbricks. We were never far from the Khabur River, one of the tributaries of the Euphrates. Without it, I would have been lost.

You, tugging my hand through the market on my day off, when the soles of my boots threatened to tear away completely. They flapped when I walked and let dust and stones in to terrorize my toes. You knew a guy, you said. Really good, really cheap. Also, he was your cousin.

The lines of disappointment around your mouth that season's first week when your sister Nadiya got the job as the team's interpreter. Her English was better and she was studying ancient history; really, what did you expect? You were barely out of school. University was an abstraction. Sometimes, as you sped us to the site in the dusty Land Rover, fiddling with the radio, glancing only carelessly at the road, I wondered if her driving was better too.

None of my memories tell me where you are now.

All the news here is bad. The TV screen fills with dusty, crying babies clutched by vengeful, helpless fathers, and I have to turn it off. I can't turn off the computer. One browser tab remains open all day, a satellite image of the tell and the town named after it, near the northern border. The number of times I refresh it indicates what kind of day I'm having. I spent four seasons excavating that tell, that mound in the desert. My fingertips know every layer, have sifted through centuries. Nearly two thousand years of continuous occupation. Now I watch it from space.

I try to call you. Do you still have the same phone or did you replace it after the screen cracked? At least it worked, though reception was intermittent. I remember people climbing to their rooftops, to the tops of hills, holding their phones to the sky, looking for a signal. Sometimes they even got one.

The day we uncovered the mosaic. The most objectively beautiful find to come from the site. Late Roman, maybe fifth century, maybe later. And just a corner, less than a square foot, had survived intact. The rest of the floor consisted of churned-up tesserae, like a million tiny chessboards shattered in the dirt. Except for this one corner, a border of stylized blue knots, an animal's raised paw. You said it must be a lion. You breathed the words. Your eyes, soft with wonder.

The tell holds a strategic position over the plain. No wonder it has been occupied so relentlessly. The Seleucids, the Romans, the Umayyads, the Abbasids. Nour, our field director, is hopeful we'll even find evidence of the Bronze Age one day.

It is spring here now. I work on the third floor of my parents' house, tapping away at the computer, typing up my field notes. The computer crouches on a low table under the eaves. I sit on wool-covered cushions on the floor, the closest copies to the ones in your mother's house that I could find. The space heater is seldom off. Yesterday I googled mosques in the city, just to know where I could go to hear the call to prayer if I needed to. There are fewer than I expected.

There were twelve of us on the dig. Many were grad students from Aleppo getting fieldwork experience. A couple, like me, were from Toronto. Plus Nadiya and you, our unofficial driver. Not too many for your mother to invite for dinner. Nadiya's girls ran around and through the gathered company, high on the excitement and novelty and the sense that no one was going to tell them off in front of guests. Nadiya's husband kept wanting to talk about the student protests in Damascus, but that verged dangerously into politics, and Nadiya or your mother managed skilfully to head him off. I saw him later, his head bent close to Nour's. They both pinched delicate blue glass teacups with the tips of their fingers. Neither of them smiling.

You lived in one of those apartment blocks the colour of sandstone that lined the highway bisecting the town. A plain rectangular block of the kind you'd see almost anywhere in the world, except for the onion-shaped opening that framed the balcony. I could just see the tops of the chestnut trees in the park around the corner, the only streak of green. The street below, leading to the busy market square, was quiet compared with the party inside. Just as the sun was retreating, the town had begun its own offensive, releasing in waves all the pent-up heat from the asphalt and concrete. My hand hovered inches from the wall, playing with it, absorbing it.

You leaned against the wall, close to my hand. You wanted to know if I had been to Palmyra. Of course I had. Before the dig began, Nour organized a trip. We drove out before dawn from Damascus to see the sun break over the ruins. We visited the Temple of Bel, and, like all tourists, I had my picture taken beside the Lion of Al-Lat. My stupid grin at odds with the lion's spiralling eyes, its bared teeth. *Al-Lat will bless whoever will not shed blood in the sanctuary*, the inscription ran.

Is it true, I asked, that there are hundreds of words in Arabic for lion?

You shrugged. Were you disappointed that I had already been there, that there was little you could still show me? Ask Nadiya, you said.

Come on. Let's get out of here. I pulled at your hand.

Every day I imagine a different scenario. The step trench on the north side of the tell, where we found the mosaic—it could be a good place to hide while rebels are shelling the town, while the rows of apartments are rendered into rubble and ash.

Or you have made it past the border, you and your family. Your wrists guiding the wheel of the Land Rover in that careless way. Your father had stuffed the trunk with boxes of the orthopaedic shoes he sells. Nadiya's girls played complicated clapping games in the front seat.

But sometimes, when I wake in the night, I see bodies dangling from street lights. They are stringing up men and boys—like in those ghastly videos online, the ones that are always "unverified"—their bodies lining the road to the covered market, which once sold phones and repaired workboots.

The trench could be nothing more than a trash pit by now, a hole to piss in, accumulating layers for future archaeologists.

The tiny scar on your lip that twisted your grin. When you were a baby, your mother fed you like she would a baby deer, dropping milk slowly into your mouth because you could not latch on properly.

Your lips were always moving, trying to suck on air. Don't be surprised that I know this. I think she liked me, your mum, even when I thought I was too old for you.

The heartbreak of archaeology is that every act of discovery must also be an act of destruction. You dig through layers, document each artifact, its position, everything you can see, and destroy it as you move deeper, further back in time. Everything relies on memory. Discoveries shift in importance, significance wavers, meanings blur as you try to translate field notes into conclusions. There are no conclusions.

Nadiya's girls thought we were digging for gold. Why else would anyone spend so much time digging holes in the ground? Gold was found there once, a hoard of coins, Seleucid, unearthed in the sixties. They ended up in a museum in Aleppo, I think. God knows where they are now.

Your breath tasted like muhammara as you drove us into the mauve night. The setting sun had struck the apartment behind us gold. It was my last night before flying home. You traced hearts on my knee. I was looking up into the sky, at the subtle variations from the purple horizon to the blackness above. The stars, beading the dome of the sky, felt as close as my own thoughts, and, for a moment, I felt like I was studying the inside of my own skull.

It was inexperience that made you drive like that, not recklessness. Just as it was inexperience when we stopped, miles past the tell, miles from anyone.

You undid your seat belt, and the vinyl seat creaked as you leaned over, as you put your right arm over my shoulder. Your eyes were already closed. Your mouth was hot. And everywhere.

Wait, I said. Stop. Are you licking my chin?

Don't you like it?

I wriggled back up in the seat and pushed you back, reversing our positions. Here, I said. Follow me.

There are carved reliefs, now in the British Museum, I think, that show Assyrian kings racing along the plain in chariots, hunting lions. They imported the lions from Africa for this privileged death. I wonder now if that's what our mosaic depicted, even though it dated from much later. A royal hunt.

On the way back, as we drove through the darkest part of the night, your hand heavy and relaxed on my thigh, there was a thump. The car went over something. Too soft to be a lump of rock. You stopped the car and got out. Your hands were shaking so much, the phone slipped from your fingers as you tried to pull it from your jeans. There was a crack as it hit the stony ground. I picked it up and stared at it helplessly. Who could I call? I needed an interpreter. I begged you to take the phone from me. But you were kneeling by the body, weeping.

The lion's eyes were open. The fur on his side was soft and warm and the colour of the desert. You ran your hands gently over his side, where his ribs protruded like the rungs of a chair's back. His front paw hung in the air, quivering. It took a long time for him to stop breathing.

Where did he come from? Is there a zoo around here?

You wiped your nose with the back of your hand. I

couldn't help but imagine the creature pursued by princes in chariots, equipped with arrows, to the point of its exhaustion. I thought of Al-Lat, of the lion's bared teeth, her magical spiralling eyes.

History collapses.

The satellite image has been updated. The tell has been bulldozed. Rows of tanks stand there now, at least twelve of them. A site of strategic importance still. Men flatten the land to show their possession of it. The space heater ticks in my blank-walled room.

We said we'd see each other again next year, though it was clear to everyone by then it would not be that soon. Men were already letting their beards grow long. Informers and militants were rumoured to be about, and it seemed the politic thing to do. But we'd be back soon, I said, grant money in hand, ready for another season. Your beard was soft, a little patchy. I rubbed the feeling of its tickle off my cheek when you weren't looking.

And then you disappeared into the desert.

Or I disappeared into the clouds.

Perhaps, any minute, my phone will ring. And perhaps it will be you. You will be standing on a Turkish hilltop, holding your phone to the sky, looking for a signal. Looking for me.

A COMPLICATED KIND OF FALLING

A SPECIAL PROVIDENCE

IT DROPS IN FRONT OF HIM SO SUDDENLY he nearly trips over it. There is no tree nearby, no roofline, nothing from which it might have lost its grip. But there it is, at his feet, alive still. Opening and closing its beak, like an actor pantomiming fear.

Kemp nudges it into his palm. The fellow's feathers are tiny. They make the ones his mother pulled from her pullets look absurdly huge. They are the colour of pebbles along the riverbed, of fresh-turned earth. And its little heart pricks his thumb, warm and rapid. Are its wings broken? He can't tell. Perhaps it had been trapped in the talons of a hawk that dropped it in favour of larger prey. He imagines its terror on the way down, its little body spiralling, too frightened to flap.

He wants to take it home, but his landlady's mouser would extend poor hospitality to a sparrow. Kemp carries him over to a budding poplar and leaves the little fellow in its arms before crossing the rest of the field to Shoreditch.

TWO GENTLEMEN OF THE THEATRE

The place still bears the scars of the cockfights from the night before. Beer and blood mix in the dirt floor of the pit, and stray feathers, blown along by the breeze through the open roof, collect along the edges of the stage. The smell of blood and death drives Crab wild. He is supposed to stand on his mark and look mournful while Kemp feeds him pieces of dried pork and delivers his lines. But Crab has other ideas.

"I'll show you the matter of it. This shoe"—*yank*—"is my father. No, this"—*yank*—"left shoe is my father. Stay, you whoreson dog, *stay*!"

Burbage, sitting on the edge of the stage and swinging one foot in the empty air, belly-laughs. "Let him go, Will. Let him get it out of his system."

He releases the rope. The mongrel dashes down the wooden stairs and, nose to the ground, snuffles in the dirt like a pig hunting for truffles.

Kemp gestures hopelessly and completes his speech. "The dog is himself. See how I lay the dust with my tears." He sits heavily, cross-legged beside Burbage. "Are you sure you want to take this one on the road? The mutt is impossible."

"Have a heart. It's his first comedy. And it's a good one to tour with, aside from the dog. Only thirteen parts and we can double four."

Kemp grunts in both agreement and annoyance.

"The boys are shaping up well. And Joan has found an excellent rose silk for Kit's Sylvia."

"Is Joan coming with us?" The company seamstress, who works backstage, who blushes in company but has the dirtiest laugh when they are alone. She has beautiful teeth; they are almost white.

But before Kemp receives an answer, their playwright struts across the stage from his perch in the tiring house.

"Will," he says. "I have some notes for you."

MASTER GENTLEMAN SHAKESPEARE

The wooden bench creaks when George Bryan drops into it. Kemp's eyes stray to the table Bryan has just left, where a man sits hunched over parchment. As he frowns in concentration, his tongue, a pink worm, darts in and out of the open hole of his mouth.

"Not Denmark again." Kemp signals to the publican for another drink.

"That dump. Audiences there wouldn't know talent if it bit them in the arse. But he keeps asking. What more can I say about the place? Cold, damp, dark. Like himself."

"Maybe he'll do us all a favour and move there."

"No chance," says Bryan. "Haven't you heard? He's applied for a coat of arms."

Kemp spits on the straw-covered floor. "They'll give it to him too. Those things are ten a penny these days."

"Doesn't your family have one?"

"My point." He calls to the publican, "Peter, what's your thruppenny dish tonight?"

BOTTOM

There is the mud, of course. Clinging to their boots in great clumps, making each step as heavy as an age. There is the sound of the complaining axle and the creak of wooden wheels on their single cart. There is the dispiriting knowledge that Coventry lies another three miles off. And there is Shakespeare buzzing in his ear. Something about conveying tragedy through a mask. Kemp will say anything, anything just to make him stop.

"An ass's head, an Italian mask, through Pyramus and Thisbe's wall, if necessary. I can play anything. But just to be clear, you've written a clown who isn't funny."

"He would be if you didn't keep changing the lines," Shakespeare retorts.

"At least I give the audience something they can understand."

"Your antics pull my play out of all shape."

Burbage from just ahead turns to them. "But Kemp's jokes are better," he says.

After a pause Shakespeare says, "We could put that ass's head on anyone, you know. No one would even know the difference."

"You're right. They won't. Nor will they be laughing."

Oh, he knows he'll be paying for it later, after they've settled into some cramped provincial tavern. He'll have to buy Shakespeare another pot of ale to smooth his ruffled feathers. It's never wise to offend the man who puts words in your mouth.

OLD JACK FALSTAFF

Kemp finds his way down through the kitchen gardens and along a narrow footpath, dodging maids and serving boys, to

Lady Montacute's ice house. Not a house, not even a building. More like a cave hollowed out from the hillside. They have stopped at this country estate on the road to Leicester, promising two plays and granted three nights' lodging.

It is dark inside and the stone floor is slippery from the wet straw. He pulls the heavy door almost completely shut, only a narrow line of light to guide him to a dry seat. There are no jokes here, no jigs. The silence settles into him.

Kemp hasn't been able to sleep. He's disturbed by dreams of sparrow feathers, by the faint strains of old Morris songs when he wakes. He misses Joan. He doesn't like to think of her alone in London, amid the long-beaked doctors who walk through pestilence in their clouds of camphor.

"Goats and monkeys! What do *you* want?"

Richard Armin, one of the hired men, a would-be clown, swings the door open with the flourish of a hero. "Rehearsal's started," he says. "The tavern scene."

When Kemp began his career, sharers were treated with respect, as befitted their senior position. All Armin ever offered him was insolence. No one likes an upstart.

"There's no play without Falstaff," he says.

Now, there's a tempting idea. No play. He dislikes Falstaff, the insufferable boor. The whole play is just a little too knowing for him. For there they are embodied in blank verse, Hal and Falstaff, Shakespeare and Kemp. Like watermen, each looking one way and rowing another. And neither appearing to their advantage.

"Just because you're a sharer, you think you can do anything. There are some who want to get rid of you, you know. And I say good luck to them." Armin leaves the door wide open. His footsteps hiss angrily across the long grass back to the house.

Kemp shivers. He has never missed a rehearsal before.

TARLETON'S CLOWN

"More salt than pepper now," she says on his return in September, fingering his curls. The theatres are about to reopen, and the players are happy to be home. "How was it?"

"The blasted dog ran away," he says, and pulls her in tight. Her hair smells of rosemary and woodsmoke. He wants to never let her go.

But there is news. Shakespeare is reworking the old *Famous Victories*. Kemp has barely seen him outside of rehearsals for weeks.

"That was Dick Tarleton's triumph. Do you remember, Joan?"

She shakes her head. "Before I came to London."

Tarleton, the Queen's favourite clown, was like sunshine when he was onstage, bright and hot and everywhere at once. But always a tricky east wind blew with him, for one never knew what kind of quip, kind or cruel, he would give next. In those early days, after Kemp practised his patter before passersby outside the Curtain, he slipped inside with the groundlings for Dick's jig. He absorbed all he could about timing, about ribald songs and performing extempore, about what pleases audiences best. They're greedy, he learned. No matter how perfect the scene or fast-paced the patter, they want more. They want better. Better than anyone can possibly give. But the player is infinitely worse. For he is greedy enough to want to be the only one to give it to them.

Kemp saw Tarleton's greatest turn just before he joined Leicester's Men. Edward Alleyn played valiant King Henry, but it was Tarleton's Derrick everyone adored.

Shakespeare has already cherry-picked from Derrick to create Falstaff. The role is already Kemp's. All he has to do is wait.

Wait.

MUCH ADO ABOUT WHITEHALL

Performing in the Great Hall the day after Christmas. Tapestried walls. Gilded ceilings. An audience similarly tapestried and gilded.

Two plays for Her Majesty, where last year they gave three. The year before, four. He tries not to think about it. He tries not to think about anything, hopping from one foot to another in the crowded antechamber where the actors prepare. He has been a clown for sixteen years and still feels the terror of a bewildered child before each performance.

"By all the saints, Will! You're trampling my gown."

Everyone thinks hair turns white with age, but it's not true. It's with fear. The Earl of Southampton spent one night in the Tower and came out capped in snow, they say. And it happens to everyone that way, only more slowly. The older you get, the more there is to fear. And there is more terror contained in the second after he delivers a joke than in all the dread-filled hours the night before battle. He should know.

Someone hisses, "Dogberry, it's you!" and Bryan slaps Dogberry's hat on his head and shoves him toward the door.

He prays to God he can still make the Queen laugh.

HENRY THE FIFTH

Every night has been colder than the last, and tonight marks the coldest. Puddles turn to ice, mud and slush freeze into unpredictable ridges to trip the unwary, and thick snow falls over everything. Kemp's knuckles are red and swollen. It must be cold like this at the end of the world.

But he doesn't stamp his feet as the others do—the players and apprentices—because that will only push the needles and pins deeper. They are all waiting for Burbage and the builder, Peter Street. Instead, he blows into his cupped palms.

Peter, a small man with a thin voice—he could never be an actor—claps his hands and shouts directions. Plank by plank, the players dismantle the stage, the tiring house, Peter marking each piece with chalk, according to some plan in his head, before they get loaded into carts and transported to a warehouse by the river. It's a clever trick. Burbage has lost the lease to the land, but the building itself belongs to the company. They will raise it again across the river. They talk as if it's a simple matter of moving the theatre, but Kemp is sorrowful. He knows it will be a different place altogether.

For a long while there is nothing but the grunts of men and the tumbling of lumber and Kemp wondering if he will ever feel his toes again. He's eavesdropping before he even realizes it.

"The new play, Will, when will I see it?" asks Burbage.

"Coming, it's coming," Shakespeare replies in his lofty way. "It's a new kind of drama. No one's done anything like this before. No clowning, no distraction. Just Hal. The man and the king."

"No clown? No Falstaff? Is that a good idea? We promised Her Majesty—"

"I have no room for Morris dancing. I'm writing for a new kind of theatre."

Burbage sighs. It is the sigh of a man who has worked with actors too long. "That's all very well, but I'd like to see some pages."

Their voices move off. Kemp kicks his foot against the wheel of a wagon, startling the horses.

Falstaff is a gentleman. A drunk and a lush too, yes, but beloved by the Queen. Kemp had been a Morris dancer. He began his career with feathers in his hat and bells on his boots. A fact not ever forgotten by some.

EXIT KEMP

He is flying. He has kicked away the cups and trenchers on the long wooden table to jig on his makeshift stage. It's easy to ignore how the table judders with every step after this much ale. People clapping, his heart thudding, they are one and the same. He could jig all the way to Norwich and back.

"Well when I was only six months old,
   the girls would handle me,
They clutched me to their bosoms and
   they bounced me on their knee,
They would rock me in the cradle, and if I made a row,
They'd tickle me, they'd cuddle me, I wish they'd do it now."

Everyone is at the Cock tonight: Bryan, Condell, Phillips, Armin, Burbage. Shakespeare. A serving girl—too tall to be pretty, but he's not fussy—gives him a wink.

"There he is," he shouts above the roar. "The man who would depose me!"

Shakespeare, engaged with Armin, half-turns to him and arches an eyebrow. Kemp hops down.

"Will—" Bryan tries to grab his arm.

"And yet there is no more valour in him than in a wild duck. You know, Will, your horse would trot better if your false promises would dismount." A tiny voice in his head wonders how this all is going to end. But it's too late to stop. He doesn't want to stop.

He sings, "Oh I wish they'd do it now. I've got itches in me britches and I wish they'd do it now." He tries to resume his jig, but suddenly he has too many feet, and they are all dancing to their own tune.

Burbage's hand on his shoulder. "No one's deposing you, Will. Falstaff just isn't in the play. We still need *you*."

Kemp shakes his head slowly, with great effort. "No, no. You will banish Kemp from the company. Banish Kemp and banish all the world."

"Never thought I'd see you quote one of my plays back at me, Will." Shakespeare is laughing. At him. Intolerable.

"Intolerable," he says, or thinks he does. He's not sure he managed all the syllables.

"George, take him home, will you?" says Burbage.

Joan will be waiting. The fire will be banked for the night. The house dark, and her frown well in place. Kemp will marry her. One day he'll remember to tell her so.

The thing about flying, it's really just a more complicated way of falling. The same rush of air in his ears. The ending, the crash, he finds, is the same. Feathers and bells.

And then he will sleep, noisily, his mouth closing and opening on empty air.

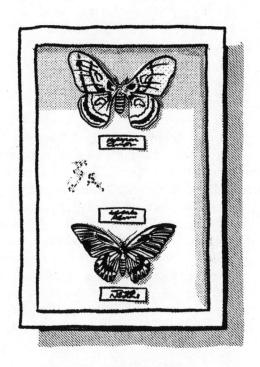

THE INVENTORY

THIS ROOM IS AS AIRLESS AS ALL THE OTHER UPSTAIRS ROOMS. The window is missing its screen, but I yank it open anyway. There are no houses or strip malls outside, only trees and the absence of traffic noise. It's like we're not in the city at all. At least the evening air dilutes the smell. Earthy, almost fetid, reminding me of the white, pudding-like feces of my brother's boa constrictor, his high school pet. I can hear Gabe moving around downstairs; he's whistling and it's reassuring, knowing he's there.

Every time I push open a door or pull open a new drawer, I expect the old man to rebuke me, to jump out of nowhere and demand to know what the fuck I'm doing. I have even more of a sense of him now, from the stubble on the bathroom sink to the bathrobe hanging from the door, smelling of old cologne—vaguely lemony—and stale sweat. Each room reveals him more, and his anger grows commensurate with my knowledge. I can almost hear his voice, slightly accented like he's from Eastern Europe, like my own grandfather. *Get the hell out of my house.*

I admire Gabe's confidence. To him this is just a job, and he goes through the house as nonchalantly as if it were his own. Not that what we're doing is wrong. Medical Services has already removed the rented hospital bed from the living room, brought in when the old man could no longer manage the stairs. The oxygen tank and the trays from Meals on Wheels have likewise vanished. Only the depressions in the carpet from the bed remain. Gabe said it was the old man's fault anyway. If he had been kinder in life, kept up with his family, then they would be here conducting the inventory instead of us.

A long wooden worktable stands against one wall, empty except for a microscope under a cracked plastic case shoved into one corner and a couple of plants in soil as dry as cereal near the window. A few withered leaves still cling to their stalks. Lining the opposite wall is a series of glass-fronted cabinets filled with trays and jars. When I open the door, there is a smell like nail polish. The old man was some kind of scientist or maybe a biology teacher. All these specimens, pickled in formaldehyde, watching me.

I peer into the trays. Heavy wooden trays with glass lids, and inside, row upon row, moths. I could understand butterflies, beautiful things with wings bright as gems. Each tray is the same though, twelve of them in total, precisely labelled and pinned. White-lined sphinx. Ipsilon dart. American copper underwing. They are the colours of white lichen on bark, of grey twigs, dead leaves. They suit my mood more than butterflies would. They suit my idea of the old man too.

Gabe is in the kitchen now. I can hear the clattering of silverware as he dumps out the cutlery drawer for sorting and counting. Gabe. If I close my eyes, I can feel his thumb on the back of my neck, firm and slow, massaging up and down, helping me relax like he did while we waited for the nurse to call my name. He has a tattoo on his left calf of a monarch butterfly, a souvenir from his favourite class in university, Death and the Afterlife. Something to do with the Day of the Dead in Mexico and the migration of monarchs. Spirits of the dead contained in butterflies. He regrets it now, but I'm glad he has it. I wish I had that kind of courage—to put something permanent on my body, to show who I am.

"You going to be okay?" he asked back in the car outside the house.

"I'm fine."

"You probably shouldn't lift anything heavy."

The moths look so delicate and soft. I unpin the largest one, on the grounds that it must be the least fragile. Possibly it's worth something. Half these species are probably extinct. It is soft, furred along its legs and antennae. Its wings, on the other hand, are made up of tiny scales, like a baby dragon. My hands must be trembling, at least a little, for the wings to move like that, to give the illusion of life. I drop the moth back into the tray and wipe the powdery residue on my jeans.

People say now how different things used to be, how a short drive in the country would result in a windshield splattered with insects. How, even in backyards in the city, the summer air could be thick with their droning. Gabe would argue that there are artificial pollinators now, that the world may be changed, but it isn't ending. It's something to talk about with him later, in the car on the way home, to mask the awkwardness.

We both agreed that now is not the time for kids. Maybe in five years. Maybe never. The world is too unsettled, for one thing. And how could we afford it? There is a part of me that hates the old man for his big, empty house with its empty bedrooms, for the times he lived in. Winters cold and decently swathed in snow. Languid summers with no evacuation notices due to air quality. He had all this and didn't share it. Didn't even protect it.

Outside, the wind's picking up. The leaves on the trees billow and hiss like they're borne on a great tide. The plants on the table tremble a little as the cool air rushes in. I retrieve my clipboard. I need to be methodical.

There, the lightest of scratches on my arm. A feeling of being pinched by a twig. The tiniest flash of movement. At my involuntary shudder, the creature, whatever it is, flies off. I keep brushing at my arm, hard, at where the pinch raised hairs, as if I could brush away the feeling from my skin, but it's spreading across my whole arm. The thing's flown up to the overhead light. The bulb is too bright for me to see the creature clearly, but its shadow is large enough, beating and fluttering against the ceiling. I can even hear a soft clicking as it beats an erratic tattoo against the glass fixture.

The rustling of the trees grows, as if a storm is heading our way. But there is something else, some undercurrent of sound from inside the room. A humming, a murmur. The lid on the first tray is askew. I try to straighten it, to let it close fully.

There's an empty space in the rows. Was there a gap earlier, a missing moth? I can't remember.

The plants under the window are shaking now, and the withered leaves are not leaves, they are pods, cocoons. The tickle spreads, spreads across my whole body. Tiny legs crawling over every inch of me.

The sound is louder now too—the humming, the rushing, the beating of wings.

The long row of cabinets, with its insect trays and reptile jars, stands between me and the door. It's vibrating now. I'll have to pass it. I'll have to see them moving, crawling about, getting ready to fly out.

Damn Gabe. Damn this house. Tears blur everything as I struggle to find my way out.

Back in the clinic, before the procedure with the awful doctor who wore a lab coat thrown over a plaid flannel shirt, I imagined what it would feel like if this bean, this conglomeration of cells that somehow produced a heartbeat before it developed a heart, kept growing inside me. As it flipped and bubbled and turned, would it feel like butterflies?

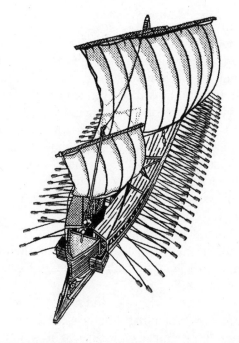

A WORD TO DESCRIBE THE SKY

WE ARE HUMBLE ARTISANS. We have no philosophical education. You won't find a Thales or a Herakleitos among our ranks. We work with our hands. Our nails are always dirty and our hours are always filled by the demands of our work, our foreman, our wives. And then Niko had to go and mess everything up.

"Hey, Philo," he says to me one day, leaning over my work so his shadow obscures the leather handle I am struggling to fix to the inside of the shield. Hektor has skimped on materials again and the leather is brittle, unyielding. My fingers are sore from wrestling with it. "What colour would you call that?" he asks, pointing upward.

"Call what? The sky, you mean?"

"Yeah."

"I dunno. Sky-coloured, I guess." Niko's breath smells like onions. I try to breathe through my mouth until he leans again over his own work. He's supposed to be polishing the thin bronze layer that covers the wood, polishing so it catches the sun and blinds the enemy with its light.

He nods slowly, chuckling and yet serious too. But Niko was like that. Never just one thing at a time.

"Sky-coloured," he says. "That's good."

But then it's the sea he can't shut up about.

"Do you want to know if there's a storm coming?" I ask. I know the water usually darkens before Poseidon unleashes his fury, but today it's smooth and calm.

"No, no," he says. "Just … can you describe it? The sea."

"Yeah, Nico," I say. "It's full of fish. Can I get back to work now, please?"

There's a large order on, and our daily quota has increased. Neither of us particularly likes Hektor, our foreman, or his filthy temper. Or the feel of his whip when his quotas aren't met.

But Niko won't stop.

"It's just that the poets call it wine-dark, don't they," he says. "Only it doesn't look anything like wine. And the sky? Hammered bronze, they call it, but"—and here he lifts up his shield—"does that look anything like the sky to you?"

I have to admit that it doesn't.

The sun starts to slip behind the hills. Time to go home. Niko and I sometimes walk part of the way together—he lives just on the other side of Diomedes' field—but I make sure to slip out quickly, barely aware of the cool wind on my overheated cheeks in my hurry. I hear him calling my name, but I don't turn around.

Myrrhine is worried. Whispers have floated up from the fishing village of foreign ships, of men speaking with strange accents landing farther up the coast. Our farmers, dressed as soldiers, not infrequently march off to battle once the crops are in, but war seldom comes to us. The news does not look good.

I tell her about Niko and his questions, mainly to distract her. She frowns, not really listening, and says she is taking the children to her father's. He lives far inland. They will be safer there.

"You can come," she says. "If you want to, you can come. You are no slave. Hektor can't make you stay."

But Hektor gives me work. I don't need to tell her this; she knows I won't leave. The simple need to provide for my family makes me stay where my work is.

It won't be for long, she promises, and kisses my cheek.

It is August now and the sea is troubled. It's not just restless and heaving, though it is that too, but it seems filled with thunderheads and wires of lightning. The riverbeds are dry, and the grass is yellow and crunches underfoot.

Foreign soldiers in dazzling fish-scale armour and pointed caps march into our village. The few of us who are left, who hadn't run from the ships and the gods' prophecies, are taken and slaughtered or merely taken. We're bundled into the hold of their ships; our captors shout at us in babbling tongues. Sometimes they slow their speech, as if talking to thick-witted children, before striking us for still not understanding them. I don't know where Niko is. I stayed behind because I thought he did too.

But I am a slave now. The strangers have placed a metal collar around my neck and leashed me to a row of other men, marched me into their ship. We sit huddled at one end, behind the foreign slaves who wield the long-handled oars. I wonder what the strangers' land is like. Will there be horn-curved oxen grazing in fields? Will they have rivers not yet drunk dry by invading armies? One day, when I have learned their terrible language, will I find they have a word to describe the sky?

It is so dark that I can barely see the others. Just the form of their bowed heads, defeated shoulders. Just the whites of their eyes.

"Philo? Is that you?"

"Niko!"

"No, it's Hektor, you fool." His voice is barely above a whisper. "We have to get out of here. Can't you feel it?"

Now I can. The boat is creaking, listing. The voices above us are urgent, the footsteps pounding the deck above our heads, hurried.

"Can you swim?" Hektor asks.

"No."

"Better stick with me then."

Suddenly he is untying the rope that binds my metal collar to the others. I don't have time to wonder, let alone ask, how Hektor got himself free. I bend toward the man next to me, the one who smells like he sleeps with goats, but Hektor grabs my arm, hisses in my ear. "We don't have time," he says.

Up on the deck, rain pelts down on sailor and slave alike, pours into our eyes. Hektor propels me to the low wall of the ship. I look down. The neat rows of oars aren't trying to cut through the swell; with the listing of the boat, they can't even reach the water. There is a splash. And another. Another. Men all around us are turning into rats.

"Quick! Follow me!"

And Hektor too is gone, vanished into the heaving broth. I lurch in the direction of his voice, I reach for the low wall, I jump—

What a fool Niko is. And all the poets. The sea is not as dark as wine. The sky is not like polished bronze. The water, the air. They are clear.

They are nothing.

CLIMBING MOUNT SINAI

BECAUSE ONE HALF OF ME IS MY MOTHER, I know she too would stand at the edge. Distinctive with her white hair swept up like an Edwardian dowager, silver bracelets rattling, taller than almost everybody else here. She would be better prepared than I am, with a bottle of Tylenol in her bag for the inevitable travel headache. She might not feel my impatience, my deep unwillingness to talk to anyone else. But she too would hang back from the rest of the tourists milling around the buses in the safe glow of the headlights.

The mountain above is unimaginable. All around me the dry, rocky valley. Like a disused quarry. It would be easy to trip or twist an ankle if I wander from the flat road.

She had been planning this trip for herself alone. Single plane ticket, single room. It had crossed my mind at first that maybe she had met someone. It was unusual for her not to travel with my father. But more than forty years of marriage made that unlikely. And the notes I found on her desk pointed to research as her aim. She had copied out sections of Exodus, descriptions of Moses's encounter on Sinai, circling certain words, the ones describing God as a cloud, as smoke, as a devouring fire.

Because I instead am here, in the country of turquoise, I am trying to see it all through her eyes.

-»»х«««-

There was never enough air. The fan was directed at her all day, but its cord didn't stretch far enough across the room to fully reach her on the bed. The highest setting was never high enough. It was a relief to leave, to get a coffee or visit the bathroom, to get away from its whine.

I graded while she slept. Or I checked my phone for emails. There were the usual spring updates from the university, reminding me to submit students' grades, informing me of deadlines by which to apply to teach in the fall the same courses I'd taught last year and the year before that.

She was hot, she said, even in her open-backed gown and with the blankets pushed down. The hospital gown was patterned with blue bubbles; inside them were the words *Please wash your hands* in French and English. I read them over and over as I ran my fingers up and down the back of her neck. *S'il vous plaît se laver les mains.* I apologized for my cold fingers.

"No," she said, from behind her curtain of unwashed hair. "It's good. Cold is good."

-‹‹‹‹‹-

At the foot of the mountain is a monastery, St. Catharine's. Its fortress-like walls enclose the gardens and several buildings, intimidating perhaps in another landscape but utterly dwarfed here by the pink granite mountain behind it.

I am only allowed to stay here because the monks remember her. Other tourists must go to the motels and inns nearby. Her Greek was perfect, an easy way to score points with these monks, and her appreciation for their library sincere—though Pahomios, the ancient monk-librarian, thought that perhaps she did not show quite enough reverence for the bush, the burning bush that once spoke with God's voice. Or for the God-trodden mountain itself, for that matter. He didn't want to criticize—he had read her article on ancient psalms in *Acta Patristica et Byzantina* and admired it—but might it be possible, could it just be, that she was lacking in faith?

She was a scholar, I said. Like me. That was her faith. And why should a daughter not follow in her mother's footsteps? Men do it all the time. Though I lack tenure and my Greek is less elegant than hers, and I'm not even sure Pahomios has understood my point.

-››‹‹-

She kept asking the time. She wasn't wearing her glasses anymore, so the clock on the wall at the foot of the bed was a meaningless blur.

When we told her, she'd always say, "Is that all?"

She tapped her right foot sometimes in time with her breathing, concentrating on keeping it even and deep, on keeping it going.

-»»<<<-

"There used to be lions on Sinai. Did you know that?" Pahomios said. "When I was a young man, I saw their prints in the snow."

"And now?"

"Now I have not seen them for many years. You don't believe me. That's okay. Sometimes I have trouble believing, myself."

-»»<<<-

Last words don't matter. Not even a little. There weren't any anyway.

-»»<<<-

I tried to nap when I arrived, but I was still too jangled from the journey, the flight into Cairo, the long bus ride through the unchanging landscape. I explored instead. I met Pahomios. The bush looked tired in the sun and rather ordinary, but I am told it is the very same one, transplanted. I preferred the other trees, the mulberry, the almond and cypresses.

There are two routes up Mount Sinai. My mother's immediate preference would have been for the older route, the less popular Steps of Penitence. She was a historian and, before I was born, an archaeologist. To her, the older version of anything was always the more attractive one. But her hips were getting stiff. Long walks were draining. Unwillingly, she would have joined the other tourists up the longer, shallower path.

Being forty years younger means I still have the luxury of choosing the more difficult way, though my knees click like grasshoppers as I climb, and they will ache and swell tomorrow.

We start at one in the morning. We'll reach the summit by dawn.

-->>)<((-

Grief had made my father accident-prone. The day after the funeral, he yanked open the cutlery drawer and it slipped right off its tracks and crashed onto his foot. The skin under the toenail is still bruised black. Later, as I was pulling dishes out of the dishwasher, I heard a shout and a distant thump. The cat, he said, had darted up the stairs in front of him, causing him to stumble. He had carpet burns on his left knee and his elbows. And even now he still won't tell me how he fractured his wrist.

So a week after the funeral I moved back home. I slipped into her old study, where nothing had been touched. Books and journals on the shelves above her desk, behind propped-up postcards and fancy bookmarks. An owl I made out of pompoms when I was seven. Her purple-rimmed reading glasses half-folded beside the monitor, the metallic cup stuffed with pens and mechanical pencils. The itinerary, near the top of a messy pile of papers on the desk. A trip for one.

I had to wait until my father's accidents subsided, for the mugs of hot coffee to stop slipping from his fingers, for the death certificate to stop giving him paper cuts.

"How're the job applications going?" he asked.

"Fine," I said, though the deadlines had all passed.

I took my last paycheque, along with most of my savings, and booked a flight to Cairo.

-<<<<<-

The path is dusty. Its steps seem made for giants. I cannot see anything of the way ahead, just what falls in the white glare of my flashlight: a tendril of dried scrub, a shiny granola bar wrapper blown against the rocks. I have never seen a blacker night, without even the smallest splinter of a moon to lighten it. I'm afraid to look beyond the beam of the flashlight, afraid I'll trip, fall into its nothingness. The wind is sharper now; my nose and the tips of my ears tingle and burn with cold. I keep switching the flashlight from one hand to the other, warming the empty hand in my pocket. The air already feels thinner. It's getting harder to speak. Harder to breathe.

I didn't expect to see lions' tracks, but there isn't a trace of life up here, not even the tiny footprints of rodents or the swish of a lizard tail in the dust. There is only the crunch of gravel underfoot and the chatter of tourists ahead, getting livelier now, the closer we get to the top.

-->>)(<<-

The platform is larger than I expected. People gather in pairs or small groups. The ones with foresight huddle under the blankets or sleeping bags they brought, sipping from thermoses. My fingers throb with cold. I stand alone at the edge. Perhaps it's because my heart is pounding from the climb, but the rounded granite rocks below, barely visible now in the faintly growing light, seem to be moving. They look like the rocky backs of leviathans shifting, cracking, reforming.

An expectant hush falls over everyone. We are waiting for dawn, for the rebirth of the world.

Only a year ago, at the beginning of the last year of her life, she planned to stand where I stand now. On the God-trodden mountain, higher than all the others, whose ridges and canyons snake out to the horizon.

The air around us turns from grey to lavender, pink, blazing orange. It tastes of the warming rock. There is the sun at last, rising from beneath our feet.

I am one half my mother. But the other half?

I concentrate on my breath, keeping it even, keeping it going.

EXPERIENTIA DOES IT

"MY OTHER PIECE OF ADVICE, COPPERFIELD," said Mr. Micawber, "you know. Annual income twenty pounds, annual expenditure nineteen nineteen and six, result happiness. Annual income twenty pounds, annual expenditure twenty pounds ought and six, result misery. The blossom is blighted, the leaf is withered, the God of day goes down upon the dreary scene, and—and in short you are for ever floored. As I am!"

To make his example the more impressive, Mr. Micawber drank a glass of punch with an air of great enjoyment and satisfaction, and whistled the College Hornpipe.

—*David Copperfield* by Charles Dickens

Nothing about St. Luke's Workhouse allowed you to forget where you were. Every mug, every spoon, the sole of every shoe was stamped with its name to keep workhouse property from being pocketed and sold on the outside. Even the glass bottles of iodine in the infirmary had the words moulded into their sides. They were the first words I learned to read, tracing my fingers over the letters on the soles of my shoes and the buttons of my dress.

They taught us reading in the workhouse. The girls got three hours of instruction every morning, going over "The Little Red Hen" and the Lord's Prayer, before we were shuffled back to the women's dormitories to learn knitting and sewing during long grey afternoons. Men and women were kept apart, except during meals at St. Luke's, and we had to be busy and useful at all other times. The matron said it was our duty. I could never figure out if the boys were more or less useful than the girls, for they spent full days in the schoolroom, learning to write and do sums as well as read.

I lived in the workhouse for seven years, from the time I was an infant. When my mother died of a putrid fever, I was kept on. There was nowhere else to go until Mr. M came. He was looking for a girl to "do" for his family. The matron recommended me for being quiet and neat and handy with a needle.

Mr. M seemed a fine gentleman. He wore a splendid blue coat—too wide in the shoulders and short at the cuffs, as if it were made for someone else, but I didn't notice this at first. I was captivated by his buttons: not one of them was stamped with words of ownership; instead they glittered with pictures of stars and crowns. His voice was kind and his manner was courteous and obliging, though I had to skip and hop to keep up with his long stride through the narrow streets to his house in Blackfriars.

The house was not large. It seemed squeezed in at the

elbows by its neighbours and forced to stretch upward in order to glimpse the sky. But it was the first proper house I could remember being in, with proper bedrooms instead of dormitories, and a kitchen, two parlours, and an attic, where I was to sleep. I could see the dome of St. Paul's from my window. The house contained more furniture then, on my first day, than it did afterwards—ponderous carved tables and chairs, damask curtains, cabinets and shelves displaying curios. It took longer to clean then as well, but I didn't mind. I was living with quality.

Mr. M hung up his coat and hat on a hook in the hall and made as if to take mine as well until he noticed I had neither. Just a plain brown wincey dress whose hem would have to be let down sooner rather than later. He led me into the front parlour, where Mrs. M sat near the window. She had finished unstitching a lace border from a handkerchief and was attaching it to a baby's bonnet. The lace was at least an inch wide and the most delicate I had ever seen, and in the inside light, it hardly looked frayed at all. A cradle lay at her feet.

"My dear," Mr. M said to his wife, "this is Mary Clickett."

Mrs. M smiled and said, "I'm delighted to make your acquaintance," just as if I were a grown-up person. I curtsied and blushed.

"Now, Mary," said Mr. M, rubbing his hands and turning to me. "You have seen our humble home and met the family. Could you see your way to adding to our domestic felicity by joining your labours to ours? Will you help us to run the household, to look after the children until they become the ornaments to society they are destined to be?"

"You're asking me to work for you?"

I was perplexed. I thought it had all been arranged. Mr. M and the beadle at the workhouse signed official-looking documents; my assent had not been required then. I hadn't yet learned that he treated everyone in grandiose style, except for his employers, of course, before whom he scraped and bowed with less inflated prose.

At his expectant look, I said, "Yes, sir."

"Splendid." He smiled and his cheeks swelled into hard little apples. His teeth were tobacco-stained, one of them chipped.

I learned quickly that Mr. M had no regular employment. Sometimes he let the bedrooms upstairs for a few shillings a week. He did odd jobs for factory owners and local merchant men—carrying messages, pasting up bills, loading stock onto carts headed to Covent Garden. More often he walked the neighbourhood with the air of a man of leisure, looking for something to "turn up." His faith that something would was enormous. Even when the deal side table or the silver coffee pot found its way to the pawnbroker's shelves in order to provide a pudding or some bread and cheese, even when the circles beneath Mrs. M's eyes darkened like bruises, he remained sanguine, hooking his thumbs into the pockets of his red waistcoat. If that waistcoat hadn't fallen deflated around his middle, he would have resembled a strutting robin.

Mr. M may not have been reliable in finding employment, but he was utterly reliable in his habits. He frequented two public houses, where he had amassed a large circle of friends. They were attracted by his gregarious, generous manner, I think. Sometimes if he stayed too late, Mrs. M would send me to fetch him home. I hated this as much for the beery stench near the entrance as for the rough attentions of the men inside.

Mrs. M liked to invite her friends—Mrs. Hargreaves, the landlady, and Mrs. Cheevers, the boot-maker's wife— for "an evening party." She would have preferred, she said, to send handwritten invitations, if only she could be quite sure her neighbours could read. Mrs. M and I melted stub ends of candles together to provide tapers for the majolica candlesticks. They guttered and dripped and never burned smoothly, but it gave the effect Mrs. M liked of having candles as long as ones bought new from the chandler's. We generally didn't drink tea for two or three days beforehand in order to have enough to offer around. She attempted to teach her friends elegant games, like faro and whist, but inevitably Mrs. Hargreaves, after having lost a hand or three, would complain that trying to read the cards made her eyes ache. Mrs. Cheevers, who never could keep the rules straight, would pull out some knitting, a bottle of whisky, and an evening's worth of gossip. I kept the children upstairs.

There used to be a third lady, a Mrs. Mott, whose husband worked in one of the factories down by Hungerford Stairs. But when he died from a fever, Mrs. Mott sold most of her belongings and moved to smaller lodgings. "Just think of the indignity of it, my dear. All her husband's clothes and her own nice gowns let go for less than half their worth," said Mrs. Cheevers, who saw no loss of dignity herself in pawing through the same shops for one of Mrs. Mott's wool skirts. "No wonder she stopped coming to our little gatherings. Lord knows how she manages to provide for all those little ones."

I stayed with the family for six years. I cleaned, cooked, mended clothes, minded the children and taught them their letters.

One night, Mr. M did not come home. I held a plate of supper back for him as I usually did, expecting a late arrival, but the fire in the stove went out, the food grew cold, and still we had no word from him. Mrs. M said I had better check in all the usual places and lent me her thick shawl. Hurrying from pool of gaslight to pool of gaslight, I went along to the offices along Thames Street, peered in the plate-glass windows of the shops, and inquired at the warehouses and factories closer to the river. I checked his favourite pubs and hovered nervously outside foul taverns. But he was nowhere.

Mrs. M was sitting up in the kitchen, pretending to sew, when I returned. Her eyes were pink-rimmed and her hands trembled, but her mouth looked resolute. I followed her example and tried darning one of the children's stockings, but the guttering candle made this difficult. I worried when Mrs. M lit a second candle. Such disregard for economy was unlike her. She placed a glass bowl of water in front of it to magnify the light on my stitches but gave up all pretense of working. I knew we were both running through the possibilities of Mr. M's fate. It seemed likely that one or other of his creditors had finally got hold of him and had him arrested. But if that were the case, surely he would have been able to send word by now?

"How much food do we have in the house, Mary?"

I got up and checked the cupboard, though I already knew. "Half a loaf of bread. Three potatoes. Flour. A heel of cheese. Tea."

"What happened to the eggs Mr. M brought home from his working for Mr. Fisher?"

"We ate the last of them last night, ma'am."

A cart rumbled through the street outside. We both waited to see if it would stop outside the house. When it didn't, she said, "And the bailiff comes tomorrow. If I sell my necklace, that might just be enough to satisfy Mr. Duggins and have a little something left over. What do you think, Mary?"

"You can't sell that necklace. It was your mother's." Not having a mother myself, I set great store by such things.

"But if I sell it, I might be able to go back to her. In the morning I must check the fare to Plymouth."

I said nothing.

"They're not real pearls, you know." She sighed. "My family didn't want me to marry Mr. M. They said he was feckless. Too poor to support a wife and lacking the talent to make any kind of fortune. We eloped. It was terribly romantic, like something out of a novel. But you see, *experientia* does it." In melancholy moods Mrs. M often lapsed into Latin.

A minute later she went upstairs and returned with a battered carpet bag, already packed. She didn't quite look at me as she said brusquely, "I have to think of the children. Please wake them, Mary, and get them dressed. The sun is coming up."

As the children ate breakfast, I was sent to the pawnbroker's with the necklace and Mrs. M's wedding ring. She had enough for the bailiff, the fare to Plymouth, and a little extra to buy food for the journey. Whether they wanted her or not, she had determined to return to her family. Her eyes burned with the prospect, her step was lighter, her voice charged with an excitement that the children soon caught. There was relief in her eyes. And hope.

"Am I coming with you?" I asked.

"You—" she began, concern clouding her features. "You will manage, Mary Clickett. You are an excellent manager. I've always said so."

So—for the first time—there was no more work to be done. I had no duty to anyone.

Mrs. M kissed my forehead, pressed some coins into my hand, and was gone.

Since the old ship's clock in the parlour had been sold the previous week, there wasn't even its ticking to ward off the silence. I would have to make a plan, find employment somewhere, new lodgings. The empty house oppressed me. From the lack of anything else to do, I trudged upstairs to bed.

Not ten minutes later, the front door banged open. "Mary! Mary! He's back! Lord help us, he's back and he needs a surgeon! Mary!"

I clattered down the stairs to find Mr. M, filthy, bleeding, hunched unnaturally between his wife and the splintered door frame. His left eye was mottled purple and swollen. Mrs. M was nearly hysterical. Eventually the surgeon came, diagnosed a couple of broken ribs, and prescribed rest. Mr. M was eased into the room's only chair. He asked in a shaky voice for some tea.

"I need some of that liquid refreshment before I can relate to my dear family the adventures of the last twenty-four hours. It is a tale to tell." But he couldn't help himself; it was half-told already before the water began to boil.

Mr. M had been on his way home from the wharf, where he heard there were jobs going, thinking to be home in time for supper. He was just crossing Carter Lane when he was knocked down by a delivery van. "I was on my back before I knew what happened. The horse had been spooked, I suppose. Probably by one of those mutts that likes to follow the butcher's boy. The van belonged to Wainwright. Livid, he was. Fired the driver on the spot. I think he took me for a lawyer or a gentleman, for he wouldn't let me move until my eyes were straight and I could remember my name and speak it clearly. Excellent man. He loaded me with apologies. And money. Look. Five pounds on condition that I wouldn't go to law. You see, my love," he added tenderly, "we have enough for Mr. Duggins now. I told you something would turn up."

I looked at Mrs. M, who was hiccupping softly. She slipped from her seat on the sofa to kneel before him and buried her face in his lap. He stroked her head fondly.

"Oh, Mr. M! I shall never leave you, my love. Never!"

I thought maybe none of us would.

"Of course you shan't, my dear," he replied consolingly. "Who would ever suggest such a thing?"

SOMETIMES A TREE

THE TREES ARE SCREAMING. Many are still a haze of bare branches, even this late in May. If I had the equipment, I would hear the air pockets form in the water column moving up their trunks, the inevitable result of prolonged drought. But my work is farther up the mountain's slope, where pines and birches tend to crowd out the aspens.

There's a noise behind me, a gasping.

My neck prickles with sweat, even in the shade of the understory. A woman, pale as birchbark, leans against a balsam fir, dragging air into her lungs. It's one of the side effects of climate change no one saw coming. Everyone knew the milder winters were allowing parasites to thrive, and the absent songbirds meant more defoliation by caterpillars. With the drought in its third year, the remaining trees are becoming increasingly maladapted to their environment.

But no one expected quite so many of them to turn back into women.

"Shhh," I tell her. "You're breathing. You are. Just relax. You're here."

It takes ages, but at last the woman's breathing begins to settle. Her heart no longer feels like a bird hurling itself against its cage, and I can stop rubbing circles on her back. She wipes tears away with her fists and straightens. She has the widest, greenest eyes I've ever seen. She's taller than me, and her arms and legs are strangely elongated—they make me think of long grasses in the wind.

"Can I call someone? Take you somewhere?"

She speaks hesitantly, like a tourist trying on a new language. "No. I'm fine. Thank you."

"Here." I dig in my pack. "Some water. I'm Lois, by the way."

She takes the bottle reluctantly. Her hands are stiff, curled into themselves like the croziers of fiddleheads. It's impossible for her to unscrew the cap.

A rush of warmth burns my cheeks, that feeling of looking after someone again. I open it for her. "What's your name?"

"Sylvie," she says.

She's so thin. All I have is my pack of saplings—white pine from the southern states—and my own water ration. No food at all. And no clothes, other than the sweater I discarded this morning, oversized on me but comically short on her. She puts it on anyway.

I have to take her back down the trail to the bus. She stumbles a little over rocks and exposed roots, so we take it slowly.

•→→→‹‹‹•

When you were ten, Margo, you sized up every tree you came across. Was it sturdy enough to climb? Did it have a branch low enough to grasp, to begin the ascent?

There was a jack pine in the park behind the community centre where I brought you every Tuesday for gymnastics class. *Pinus banksiana*. Its branches stuck out like the rungs of a ladder and its curling tip waved over the roof. The tallest tree in the park was always irresistible to you. All I could see was your favourite crimson T-shirt rising like a flag up a ship's mast. Occasionally an arm stuck out from the bristle-brush branches and waved. Other parents stopped, marvelled, gave dire warnings. I could only breathe again when you were back on earth, sap smearing your shorts, a hitchhiking spider in your hair. How matter-of-factly you plucked it out.

-》》X《《-

When Sylvie and I reach the bus, I text Tom. The door is unlocked, so I can borrow a spare T-shirt and shorts from one of the other planters, but without the keys, we'll have to wait until everyone returns before we can enjoy the air conditioning. There are six of us out here today, members of Regreen & Renew, volunteers connected with the government's program for assisted migration. But sitting with Sylvie in the bus's rectangle of shade, gazing at the sparkle of sunlight on the water through the pines, it feels like we're the only two people left in the world.

Tom's good with these girls. Mostly they fall in love with him. I'd fall in love with him too if I didn't remind myself every morning I could be his mother. He takes them out, acclimatizes them to being with people again. I asked him once where he takes them; mostly they go for drinks at the Royal Oak. There's not much else to do around here.

A pileated woodpecker drills nearby, sharp-beaked and insistent.

"Does it hurt?" I touch her stiff fingers, half expecting them to shrivel into themselves even more. Sylvie shrugs. "Is it arthritis?" Grandpa had arthritis, but his claws looked nothing like this. "Maybe you should see a doctor."

"No." She pulls away. "No doctors. I'm fine."

My turn to shrug. "Suit yourself."

Hands are unnecessary, she explains eventually. They're a flourish, like the curlicues in fancy calligraphy. The real tools for survival are in her feet.

Only she calls them roots.

-»»«««-

I've had almost a year to put it together, Margo, the events of that night, from some of the people who were there and from everything you didn't say.

Why didn't you tell me? In your tree-climbing days, you told me everything.

A party by the lake. End of term. You said it was just friends from school. I had no idea where it was, that it was so close to our old sugar bush. You were almost home. But in the dark, in the unfaithful firelight that deepens the surrounding shadows, it was strange and new. Somebody brought a keg. Beer circulated in red plastic cups. Music drowned out the sounds of the night, the hooting owls, the coyotes. Maybe there were more people you didn't know than people you did. Students taking a break from tree planting. Newcomers from the drowning Maritimes.

But even people you know can become unrecognizable in the shifting orange light.

The snap of a twig from behind you. A body blocking your escape. Hands coming out of the dark, pushing you to the ground.

How I wish you could have scrambled through the brush and found safety among the trees. But not everyone is so lucky.

At least Tom was there to bring you home.

-->>)(((--

A text from Tom.

"He's on his way," I tell Sylvie. "You'll like him. He was one of my grad students. He's good at looking after people, even got me involved with Regreen & Renew."

This job was supposed to keep me from brooding. I thought there might have been some kind of redemption in my sunburned cheeks and nose, in my aching knees.

Tom used to help me with my research, testing how quickly the mycorrhizal network sent messages—chemical warnings of approaching danger—from tree to tree.

I never thought, until now, of simply asking.

"What was it like?"

"Pardon?"

"Being a tree. Did you and the other trees—communicate?"

She cocks her head. "I could feel them. They could feel me. We helped each other. It was like ... buzzing? No, humming. We hummed together."

-->>)(((--

Before you left, it was becoming clear the Ottawa Valley was only going to get hotter and drier. I talked about moving. If we moved up north, where it used to be too cold to contemplate winter, we could just about keep the climate we were used to. Yes, there were blackflies and terrible roads and even more expensive groceries. But we could have our own sugar bush again. My grandparents' bush was already dying, barely producing enough sap for family use. I had stopped tapping completely. The trees needed it more.

You rolled your eyes.

I had a lot of plans for us and they usually involved some kind of running away, lighting out on our own, just us two. But you didn't want to leave then; you had friends here, a life.

-⇒⇒⟨⟨⟨-

Tom comes huffing down the path toward us. He's wearing the same white Montreal Jazz Festival T-shirt he used to wear as an undergrad, worn gossamer-thin now and providing barely any protection against the sun.

"The others will be here soon," he says, and smiles at Sylvie. He notices what I didn't—an ant struggling up her long hair, and pinches it away.

"Sylvie's staying with me tonight," I say. "I've got a pullout."

She looks at me. "A pullout?"

"My couch folds out into a bed."

Tom, the only one with a license to drive a bus, sticks the key in the ignition and turns up the air conditioning. We climb on after him.

-⇒⇒⟨⟨⟨-

You can tell most easily with quivering aspens. *Populus tremuloides*. Entire stands of them can be genetically identical, connected by a communicating root system. They're practically one organism, and if left undisturbed, they can live for hundreds, maybe thousands, of years. But in cases where the grove dies, from drought or disease, one or two trees may remain. Not flourishing, but dutifully pushing out the bare minimum of leaves each spring. There are support groups gathering now around these outliers, but it's not an exact science.

Sometimes a tree is just a tree.

-》》✕《《-

Sylvie fits into your clothes so easily that for a second my eyes blur, for a second you are home again. But this never was your home, this one-bedroom apartment with the parking lot view. Your clothes, the ones you left behind, smell of the cardboard box I packed them in. The spare sheets smell like cardboard too. She crouches in front of the bookcase. All of your old books are there, paperback thrillers mostly, a couple biographies of your favourite singers—Lou Reed and David Bowie—travel guides from that year you spent travelling after high school. She pulls out *The Rough Guide to Thailand* and runs her fingers over its bright cover.

"Lois?"

I am staring.

"Mmm. Fine. Tom's coming by later. He wants to take you out for a drink."

There's hardly any natural light in the apartment, and by mid-afternoon it's already growing dim. I click on the light so she can read better.

I was always doing that.

-》》✕《《-

You were always going to leave. That was the deal, the one every parent knows from the beginning. But I was not prepared for the silence you left behind. How unforgiving it was.

Tom and I had been testing the network, measuring how quickly and how far one tree could send out reserves of carbon and nitrogen to aid another in distress. In this case it meant injuring the trees ourselves, lopping off branches of some of the specimens of maple we planted last year. A long and difficult day. Tom was hungover. I had to snap at him for his sloppy note-taking and then awkwardly apologize later as we drove back to the city. I remember stopping on the way home for takeout to surprise you. Egg rolls and crispy beef, moo goo gai pan and lemon chicken. All our old favourites, to tempt you out of your new reticence.

You were already gone. Your guitar and most of your clothes. How matter-of-factly you plucked yourself out of my life.

-》》X《《-

The meteor shower is my idea. Sylvie never has much energy, but now she's growing listless. She stands in front of the sliding glass door to the balcony, practically motionless, for hours. It's not just the heat. It's not the process of adjustment. It's the acres of asphalt and cement in the city. It must be, because I feel it too. There's a sick-looking Douglas fir that blocks almost all natural light from the living room struggling on in its small patch of lawn. I think she's keeping it company. We need to get out of here.

Tom hasn't been around in a few days, and I wonder if he and Sylvie had an argument. They're both so careful not to mention each other's names. His voice is wary when I call, but when I suggest the trip, he pounces on the idea. Thank goodness, because we need to drive miles from the city to get away from the light pollution and the heat. I still don't have a car.

⊸⟨⟨⟨⟨⟨⊷

I used to wish you and Tom would get together. He's only a couple of years older. He's bright. And he'd keep you close to me.

You wanted nothing to do with him. You said there was something sleazy in the way he looked after the girls from the woods. And then, after the party, you refused to mention him at all.

It was easy to pretend not to notice.

It was safer.

⊸⟩⟩⟨⟨⟨⊷

There are a couple of other cars here, in the small gravel parking lot designated a Dark Sky Zone. Sylvie draws away from Tom's car to the tall grasses, to the edge of the wilderness. If possible, she looks even thinner than when I found her. The moonless night is loud with cicadas and the high whine of mosquitoes. Almost immediately my skin feels like it is crawling with insects.

"Hang on, I've got some bug spray." Tom limps round to the trunk and rummages around inside.

"Tom, what's wrong with your foot?"

"It's nothing."

I can barely make out the other people here. Some are standing by their cars; others have moved out to the edge of the lot. They are like shadows, as still and silent as Sylvie, all of them gazing in expectation to the northeast. The air is thick and humid and tinged with the smell of wet wood, of something rotting.

I lower my voice. "No, really. What happened?"

"Splinters. Should've put some shoes on, I guess. Found it!" He brandishes the plastic bottle.

"Splinters?" I ask too loudly. There is a shushing from the shadows, from the other stargazers.

"Don't laugh," he whispers.

He was able to remove three of them, he says, but the rest are too deeply embedded. But wood's organic and so is he. They'll dissolve eventually.

"What were you doing to get the splinters in the first place?"

He glances at Sylvie, whose back is toward us.

I try to make out his expression, to work out what he's not telling me. But now that the interior light from the car has turned off, there is only the Milky Way above us and the intermittent blinking of fireflies, out earlier than ever this year, to see by. Tom is invisible. All I see is a tall, blocky figure moving toward Sylvie. A hand reaching out of the dark.

I can't look away anymore. I can't pretend not to see.

I remind myself that we are surrounded by people. Even if they seem as self-contained as a forest, they are still here. I am not alone. I step forward, blocking his way.

"You should go."

"What?"

"Go home, Tom. You need to leave us alone." I am not whispering anymore.

"Lois, you can't be serious."

I pull out my phone. "I'll call the police if I have to."

People are turning, watching us. Sylvie's hand slips into mine. Her stiff fingers wriggle and uncurl, just a little. Air pockets move just below the surface of her skin.

She is still screaming, but now, at last, I can hear her.

"We'll find our own way home. Without you."

-->>>X<<<-

The stars are so close out here, their suspension in the black sky such a tenuous thing. One swift breeze and they'll scatter like snow. I miss you so much it's hard to breathe.

This time I promise, Margo, I promise I won't let go.

THE STONECUTTER'S MASTERPIECE

WHEN SHE APPEARED, a half-veiled figure slowly coming down the road, he thought she came with a commission. No one else ever came down into this Pembrokeshire valley. His workshop was the only thing in it, curled at the bottom of it like a sleeping cat.

As she approached, the stonecutter saw she wasn't veiled at all, just wrapped sensibly against the cold. She wore a scarf over her hair, a plain mackintosh, an ankle-length wool skirt. Her hands were gloved, and she wore heavy, sensible shoes, which dragged and drew grooves in the gravel road as she walked. The only part of her that remained uncovered was her face, which was pale and finely lined.

He took in her eyes bruised by tiredness, the slight hunch. She was younger than he was, late forties perhaps, early fifties. Patience on a monument, he thought. He gestured to the only seat, a white plastic lawn chair, and offered tea from his flask. There was a grinding sound, like mortar against pestle, as she lowered herself down.

"We've met before." Her accent was foreign, vaguely Scottish. It was pleasing, the way it tumbled gently around her mouth like pebbles down a rock slip. "You replaced one of the gargoyles on our battlements. Ashworth House."

That had been a good job, taking him away from Pembrokeshire and the gravestones that were his bread and butter, a job that required no skill beyond spelling the departed's name correctly. Plus, the National Trust had paid surprisingly well.

"Mrs. Adams, isn't it?"

"Yes."

"Another shaky gargoyle?"

She cupped the mug of tea in her fingers but didn't lift it to her lips.

"I'm not a trustee anymore. I've retired."

She paused and looked around—from the workshop around her, the rubble on the ground, the chisels and mallets lying on the wooden table, the raised garage door exposing them to the elements —as if gathering in her next words.

"Do you need to see the shape in the stone before you start chipping away at it? Does the stone tell you what it is, what it wants to be?" she said.

She spoke with such directness, yet the stonecutter couldn't guess at her real meaning. He leaned against the workbench, wishing he had more than one chair. He wasn't used to visitors.

"That's not how it works," he said. "You have to work from a model. I sculpt the subject first in clay." He talked as if this was something he still did, as if he were still a sculptor, an artist, not just the local stonemason. It felt good to talk this way.

Strands of steam danced up from her tea, blurring her features. "Couldn't you shorten the process by going to the stone first and last?"

There was something about the determined way she asked, like someone with a stutter forcing the words out. As if his answer would mean everything to her. He shrugged. "It's possible."

"I really didn't know who else to ask."

She handed the mug back to him just as a gust of wind blew through the valley. It lifted her skirt slightly, and he glimpsed, above her shoe, the coarse grain of granite.

It had started with her feet, she told him. With cracks in her heels that she thought were just dry skin. A vaguely greyish tone that she thought was a sign of poor circulation. Rock dust in her sheets when she woke in the morning. Freckles on her arms that shimmered like grains of quartz. Then her knees started to grow lumpen, inelegant, bending her legs in unnatural angles, grinding with every movement. She lifted her skirt to show him. She'd had such nice legs before, she said. Strong legs.

"Can you help me?"

-→→)(←←-

Before he accepted, he would have to see her. All of her. That was his condition. He would never accept a delivery from a quarry without inspecting it first.

The wind blew through the valley again, and with it, a cold spattering of rain. Automatically he started putting away his tools, protecting them from moisture and rust. In movements almost as automatic, she began to undress. There was that sound again, the grinding of mortar and pestle. Her movements were slow, laboured, but she displayed no sign of shame or embarrassment or even cold. When he turned back around, there she was.

"This is not really me," she said. "It's more like—a shell."

She was a woman assembled from boulders. The hair on her head grew in patches; in places where she was bald, skin had turned to rock. Unmoving breasts overhung a cold grey belly. Thighs that were practically egg-shaped showed signs of erosion where they rubbed together.

"Every day I change a little more."

He reached out. "Do you mind—" But he didn't wait for her consent. His hands were on her, feeling the rock, sliding over its surface, sometimes smooth, sometimes pitted. He was measuring her with his fingers first before he brought out the calipers. Learning her. She was something between a bluestone and something much softer, like marble, he thought. She was like nothing he had seen before.

Mrs. Adams fixed her gaze on the horizon.

The stonecutter dropped his hands from her body. There were spots of rain on his glasses, and his breath released small puffs of fog between them. He nodded slowly. He folded his arms, took a step back and nodded again. It must also have been rain that wetted her cheeks.

"When do you want to start?" he asked.

-->>)<((--

The project excited him; he couldn't deny it. It brought back that rush of feeling he remembered from his long-ago twenties, when he had first toured the marble workshops of Florence and Rome. When his ambition still surpassed his skill and nothing surpassed his expectations.

He didn't even bother with the point chisel since the general shape was already there. He had visions of the Nike of Samothrace, how its ancient carver had created delicate folds of fabric, gauze out of rock, that fluttered and moved and revealed the body beneath. He started with a flat chisel. The stonecutter could see, emerging beneath his hands, the delicate weave of cloth, the smoothness of thigh.

There was a dry rumble that might have been a groan.

"Are you all right?"

"I'm fine." Her voice sounded like it was coming from far away, yet he could feel the vibration of it in the cool rock beneath his hands. "It's fine."

"Do you want me to stop?"

"No. It only hurts a little. Go on. Go on."

He proceeded more slowly. He tried to be gentle, but how can you chisel and crack and chip away gently? His chisel sang against the stone, as clear and light as a bell.

She stood straight, arms at her sides like a caryatid or one of those simple Egyptian funerary statues. But he would cut movement into her. Her clothes would blow against her body, her face would tilt upward and give a Mona Lisa–like smile to the sky. He had in mind something classical. A vaguely toga-like garment. Leather sandals on her bare feet. She might adorn a pagan temple.

It could take weeks, months perhaps. He set up several work lights to extend his working hours. He felt guilty when he stopped to rest, to sleep in the cot he kept in the back of the workshop or to have a bite of something, while she stood motionless outside. Within days her metamorphosis was complete and she was all stone. Movement was impossible. Her gaze was fixed upward, as if she were an augur and, having mapped out the sky, was waiting for a message to fly across it. He could hear gulls sometimes—they weren't that far from the sea—and ravens, though he rarely saw them.

They talked as he worked. Though her lips and jaw had hardened into stone, her voice floated through his mind. He smoothed away the corrugations made by his toothed chisel, the grooves in her forehead, the wrinkles in front of her ears. His rasp against the stone sometimes sounded like a whisper.

He found himself telling her about the long-ago years of his apprenticeship, about the first time he saw Canova's Cupid and Psyche and what a revelation that was. He travelled back over years. And beneath his hands, she grew younger too. Her hair was now gathered in tendrils along her neck, her dress in folds beneath her breasts, along her hips. He was no Phidias, but he wasn't bad. He could make something that would last. She helped him believe in himself again.

Christmas came, and he draped gold tinsel over her shoulders and toasted her with rum and eggnog. At her request, he played carols on his small radio. The sound was terrible, tinny and small, but she didn't seem to mind. She hummed along in his mind. Her voice was deeper, more resonant than he remembered. She liked the old carols, "The Holly and the Ivy," "Greensleeves."

But after Christmas she spoke less and less. It was the beginning of February when he finished and he'd almost forgotten the feel of her voice floating through his head. The stonecutter brought a full-length mirror from his apartment. She was a Greek goddess, ageless and beautiful. Her wrinkles were gone, her hunch smoothed away. He felt silly holding the mirror up to a statue, asking what it thought.

Silence at first.

And then a small voice, like the finest grade of sandpaper. *This is not me.* It repeated, *This is not me.*

And grew louder, rising to the roar of an avalanche. *This is not what I meant at all!*

"Oh, isn't it?" the stonecutter growled. He had poured months of work into this; he had turned down paying commissions to complete this—what he knew was his masterpiece, his highest achievement.

He hurled the mirror to the ground, and it smashed against the concrete floor.

But it was not destruction enough. All that work, months and months, the utmost of his skill. Whoever heard of carving a life-size statue without even using a plaster model? He did not get it wrong.

The stonecutter snatched up a hammer and chisel from his tool bench.

Her nose came off with one hit. Her ears too and her graceful fingers. Whack, whack, whack. His chisel didn't sing against the stone. It stuttered. It raged. He gouged out chunks from her head, her torso, circling and pounding at random. His beloved drapery crumbled.

When he had finished, when he fell to his knees amid the rubble, pink-faced and panting, she was no longer a woman. Certainly not the most beautiful figure he had ever carved. A blocky head, a vague torso, still oddly supported by perfectly chiselled sandalled feet. Barely human.

Show me.

He raised his face from his hands. "What?"

Show me. The voice was urgent.

He picked up a long mirror shard, careful of its sharp edges.

Yesssss, she sighed. *Finally.*

Lumpen and disfigured. He couldn't bear to dwell on the result of his destruction. Where the chisel had broken pieces away, her inner porphyritic texture was revealed, rough and uneven, in all the colours of the earth. He looked away.

"You look like a ruin."

Finally, she said in his mind, *I look like myself.*

-‹‹‹‹‹-

It was the last thing she ever said to him.

He walked carefully around her, avoiding her gaze as he cleaned his tools and swept the floor. Eventually he grew tired of attempting awkward, one-sided conversations. Of half-apologies. And after a while, after many days, he even began to wonder if he had only ever imagined her voice, her original commission. The whole thing was absurd. Distasteful.

Her presence filled him with shame.

He had a girlfriend from Canada once, an Arctic researcher, and he lived with her in Nunavut for one sunless winter. It was there he first saw an inuksuk. A real one, not one of those kitschy fibreglass things people put in their gardens. It was only about four feet tall, a figure of a man made by piling rocks together. Its arms stuck straight out, like a child's drawing of a stick figure, but with one arm much longer than the other. She told him it was indicating the direction to the nearest settlement. He never forgot that. That empty land, draped in cold, populated by stone people pointing the way home.

The stonecutter draped her in blue padded blankets, tied them around with thin yellow rope for the journey. She was almost too heavy for him to manage on his own. He heaved and pushed and grunted and tipped her onto the dolly, then into his truck. He was thankful for the violent hewing he had done; the removal of that extra weight was necessary for him to get her even this far. He drove out of his valley, from which he'd always had to look up to see the horizon, and headed for the Preseli Mountains.

He untied the ropes, pulled the blankets away in a flourish. She still looked terrible, like something that had erupted from the raw earth. He turned her. Turned her again, one more inch, so she might face west, the direction of the sea. Her quartz-freckled body glinted in the sunlight. Her sandalled feet flattened the grass and dug into the ground. There were others like her here, standing stones. She would not be alone.

He hoped she would say something, some word of acknowledgement, of farewell. He hoped he'd hear something beyond the sound of the wind and the gulls crying overhead. He wanted to know he had done the right thing.

The stonecutter climbed back into his truck. He thought, with regret, of her finely lined eyes. Of his now-empty workshop.

Overhead, the sky changed and changed.

ACKNOWLEDGEMENTS

A sincere thank you to the team at Invisible Publishing for treating this book with such care and attention. Thanks especially go to Bryan Ibeas, who championed it and also made it immeasurably better with his thoughtful edits, and to Megan Fildes for her beautiful cover and design work.

For publishing earlier versions of these stories, and for the guidance of their editors, I'm grateful to *Agnes and True, Timeworn Literary Journal, Historia Magazine, Whispering Gallery, Stonecoast Review, The Cabinet of Heed,* and *The Weight of Feathers: a Retreat West anthology.*

Thanks to Sarah Selecky and her online Writing School. Some of the stories in this collection had their genesis in the lessons and exercises of its Story Intensive.

And lastly, thanks to all my family, but especially to Chris and Nick, for their unflagging support and encouragement.

INVISIBLE PUBLISHING produces fine Canadian literature for those who enjoy such things. As an independent, not-for-profit publisher, we work to build communities that sustain and encourage engaging, literary, and current writing.

Invisible Publishing has been in operation for over a decade. We released our first fiction titles in the spring of 2007, and our catalogue has come to include works of graphic fiction and nonfiction, pop culture biographies, experimental poetry, and prose.

We are committed to publishing writers with diverse voices and experiences. In acknowledging historical and systemic barriers, and the limits of our existing catalogue, we strongly encourage writers from LGBTQ2SIA+ communities, Indigenous writers, and writers of colour to submit their work.

Invisible Publishing is also home to the Bibliophonic series of music books and the Throwback series of CanLit reissues.

If you'd like to know more, please get in touch:
info@invisiblepublishing.com